I Want to Watch

Diego de Silva is the author of two acclaimed novels, *Certi Bambini* and *Voglio Guardare* (*I Want to Watch*). This is his first book to be published in English.

Diego De Silva

I Want to Watch

Translated by Shaun Whiteside

arrow books

Published by Arrow Books 2008

2 4 6 8 10 9 7 5 3 1

Copyright © Diego de Silva 2001

Translation copyright © Shaun Whiteside 2007

Diego de Silva has asserted his right under the Copyright, Designs and Patents Act,
1988 to be identified as the author of this work.

First published in Italian under the title *Voglio Guardare* by Giulio Einaudi Editore,
Torino, Italy in 2001

First published in Great Britain in 2007 by
William Heinemann
The Random House Group Limited
20 Vauxhall Bridge Road, London, SW1V 2SA

www.rbooks.co.uk

Addresses for companies within The Random House Group Limited can be found
at: www.randomhouse.co.uk/offices.htm

The Random House Group Limited Reg. No. 954009

A CIP catalogue record for this book
is available from the British Library

ISBN 9780099468301

The Random House Group Limited supports The Forest Stewardship Council
(FSC), the leading international forest certification organisation. All our titles that are
printed on Greenpeace approved FSC certified paper carry the FSC logo. Our paper
procurement policy can be found at www.rbooks.co.uk/environment

Typeset by SX Composing DTP, Rayleigh, Essex
Printed and bound in Great Britain by
CPI Bookmarque, Croydon, CR0 4TD

And if something of his obsession taints the day-to-day transactions of his life, but does not fully enter into them, it is like the shade of night when it hangs upon the walls of a house but does not enter it or alter it.

Alfredo De Marsico, Speech in defence of the schoolboy Pasquale Pugliese, Court of Rome, 1 April, 1941

1

The coast road smells of restaurants and burning. There aren't many cars around at four o'clock in the afternoon. The sea is there, but you can't hear it. The billboards are all blue eyes and straight teeth and crossed thighs.

Beneath the poster for a local radio station – a woman's face obscured by a pair of big sunglasses, her hand touching the dial, her lips parted – Celeste waits.

She's sixteen, and her body's pretty average. Neither short nor thin. She often wears a bandana to cover her hair. No skirts, no coats. No make-up, apart from a bit of eyeshadow. She's in her fifth year at secondary school, specialising in sciences.

Today she's looking up at the sky. She knows that colour. It's about to rain, heavily. That rotten rain that bleaches your clothes, and leaves a thin layer of sticky brown dust on the cars (you often see people wiping down their windows with tissues before they set off, because windscreen wipers only make it worse).

Celeste sniffs the air, peers into it, sticks out her tongue and tastes it, touches a finger first to one cheek, then to the other, as though by testing the way the moisture sticks to her skin she can tell how long it will be before it starts to rain.

She never pauses to think about these things she does, or whether there's any point, any sense to them. She just does them. She hasn't learned these things from anyone, she's never told anyone about them.

She runs her index finger over her face again, to just below her eyes, then inspects the tip of her finger, rubs it delicately against her thumb as though analysing a clue, or mixing together the elements of some kind of material. She reckons that she'll just about get home in time, give or take. She doesn't live far away. On the other hand she doesn't feel like going home. She lets her Invicta backpack slide onto the pavement, and then sits on it carelessly. She draws her knees up under her chin and wraps her arms around them. She taps out a rhythm with her toes.

It's the second time the green Uno has driven past. The guy inside is sweating with shame, still battling with his dignity, unable to make a decision. He knows – boy does he know – that he's been spotted. And he's acutely aware that the longer he lets it go on, the worse it's going to be. He drives as though he's left the handbrake on. The flush on his face has reached his forehead, and it's still rising. He passes close by Celeste again, he doesn't even slow down, but just glances at her for a moment and drives on, like the twat he is.

Celeste watches after him as his engine hums. He looks at her in the rear-view mirror. His face is repressed and miserable. Oh, come on, thinks Celeste. If you want to turn around now, you're going to have to go through the tunnel, sit in all the traffic on the other side and then drive half the length of the coast road in the opposite direction. At the very least it's going to take you another twenty minutes, even half an hour.

'He had a hairpiece.' says Celeste, out loud. And she starts tapping out the rhythm with her feet again. This time she sings.

It starts to rain. Celeste adjusts the knot of her bandana. Only the odd drop of rain so far, she can sit here for a while yet, then she'll go and wait under the bus shelter. She lifts the collar of her denim jacket and buttons it to the top.

Another car drives by. Young, this one, clean-looking, a tennis player, bushy hair, cotton sweater, no shirt, one of those bodies that are always so lightly dressed, those bodies for which it is always spring, the eyes that size things up, register preferences. The car is old, but like the man himself there's something experienced about it that draws the eye (Celeste imagines it in summer, sand on the seats, double-parked by a bar with tables outside, late in the evening, waiting for a group of young people to settle on where they're going).

He drives past her. He looks at her so intently it makes her wonder if he would actually ask her what she was up to if he was walking.

Celeste smiles without returning his gaze. She's used to this kind of incredulity. Other people can't quite get their heads round it. The penny doesn't drop until they've driven past, and by then it's too late. And she always recognises them when they come back.

So many times Celeste has spotted them from a distance, protected by their cars, that precise shake of the head, both disapproval and impotent resignation.

She stands up as the rain gets heavier. Maybe she'll be able to get herself picked up before she reaches the bus shelter. She sticks out her thumb.

The first one doesn't even notice. He keeps both hands on the wheel, his eyes narrowed to slits. The rain must be making it hard to see.

The next one's a woman.

The third looks at her with the usual expression of astonishment.

The one after that pulls up.

'Am I right in thinking . . .?' he asks, lowering the window.

Celeste, hands in her jacket pockets, leans forwards and sizes him up. As he waits for her reply, he moves towards her slightly as though trying to get her into focus.

He must be a little over fifty, his tie snaking down his belly, big fat hands, the usual expression of embarrassment on his face, but he's well dressed.

Clean-looking.

Polite, from the way he asked.

And the car smells new.

2

Giggling, the little girl hurtles down the corridor of the high-ceilinged apartment. She runs as though running from a tickling, a feeling that grows more intense the harder she plays at getting away from it. She jiggles and squeaks, throws herself exaggeratedly forwards with her arms dangling, slaps her hands in the air, instinctively aware that she might fall over, yet excited to the point of intoxication by her own uncoordinated movements.

From the doorway leading onto the corridor, the man watches her.

The little girl throws her head back, gauges the distance between them, and gives him a look as if to remind him of the terms of the chase. She smiles at him and stops dead. She clenches her fists, bites them and sets off again.

The man keeps his part of the bargain.

Towards the sitting room, the corridor narrows to a funnel, a little corner that is barely illuminated by the yellowish light through the curtains. The little girl falls forwards, still giggling. She doesn't bother to get up, and instead comes into the room on all fours. She is making an appealing little noise, toneless syllables, all sound and saliva.

The man walks on.

The room is divided down the middle by a three-seater sofa, with two armchairs facing it: this side for dinner (table, chairs and a small sideboard), that side for conversation. The little girl crouches down behind the back of the sofa.

The man arrives, stepping carefully. Kneeling, the little girl presses her fists under her chin and stifles a peal of laughter. Exaggerating the sound of his movements, the man looks everywhere. Behind the curtains, the door, around the television, under the carpet. Finally he walks over to the sofa, careful not to be seen above the back. The little girl crams her hands into her mouth. The man takes the cushions off the sofa, calls the little girl by name, asking her where on earth she's got to. Once. Twice. Three times. Then he gives in.

The little girl bursts from her hiding place like a jack-in-the-box, with a squeal of delight. The man pulls a startled face, puts his hands on his sides, the loser of the game, leans his head to the side, raises his eyebrows and turns down the corners of his mouth. The little girl slaps the back of the sofa, jumping on the spot. Then she comes round and hurls herself at the man, hugging his waist. He kneels down and puts his hands on her shoulders. The little girl throws her arms around his head. The man hears the girl slowly getting her breath back. He kisses her brow and the top of her head. He strokes her back, then wraps his arms around her.

The little girl's breath quickens slightly. She takes her hands off the man's head and tries to move. She manages to do so, but only after a moment. It isn't the fluid line of a free action, moving from one place to the next as she's used to; rather it's a vague sense of impediment, of hindrance, an underhand intention, a purpose concealed. She's gripped by a fear that she has never felt before, which immediately turns liquid and spills from her eyes. She tries to find the man's face. He smiles at her, but his lips are trembling. The little girl looks at him guiltily, as though to ask forgiveness for something she doesn't think she has done. The man presses one arm behind her back and with his other hand grips her hair. The little girl doesn't try to break free, she trusts him, accepting that she deserves a punishment even though it makes no sense to her. The man holds and pulls. A single manoeuvre in two opposing directions. Immediate and expertly done.

The sound of the breaking neck is like the snapping of a taut string. But what is more terrible is the creaking sound that follows, delicate and helpless.

The man gnaws his lips. He finds relief in the sudden lightness of the body, finally freed from tension. He lays the little girl on the sofa cushions, strokes her forehead and looks into her eyes, which are still stunned with horror. He rises to his feet. He leaves the room, walks back down the corridor and goes into the kitchen. He washes his hands with washing-up liquid in the sink. He dries them with a piece of kitchen paper, screws it up and throws it into the rubbish bin. He puts an espresso pot, already full, on the stove. He sits down at the table and waits, his head bowed as though with shame. After a few moments he gets up again, opens both cupboard doors, and spoons large amounts of sugar into an empty cup. He pours out the coffee, which has by now reached the rim of the pot. He drinks it down in one, with a sharp jerk of his head and tearful exhaustion in his eyes, like a pelican gulping down an unusually challenging fish. He feels the heat and welcomes it, waiting for his clenched hand to relax. He rinses the little cup in the sink, dries it and returns it to the cupboard. Without looking, he opens the door under the sink, reaches inside, pulls out a black binbag, scrunches it up as small possible and slips it into a trouser pocket. Then he goes back into the sitting room.

The girl is where he left her, her arms dangling, her hands slightly open, as though miming childbirth or salvation. The man picks her up, carries her into the bedroom, lays her out on the sheets, undresses her and then himself. He carefully folds both his clothes and his underwear and the little girl's, and slips them into the black plastic bag that he has taken from his pocket. He puts the bag on the floor. He goes into the bathroom next door. He turns on the tap in the bath. From a little cabinet he takes a pair of scissors, a bottle of talcum powder and a pair of plastic medical gloves wrapped in polythene. He places the bottle and the gloves on the edge of the basin. He cuts his fingernails. He gathers the cuttings in two folded sheets of toilet paper, throws the ball of paper into the toilet and flushes. He puts on the gloves. He goes back into the bedroom. He picks up the little girl, moving slowly as though he fears waking her.

He holds her arms to keep them from dangling. He carries her into the bathroom. He slips her into the bathwater. He turns off the tap. He returns to the bedroom. From the chest of drawers he takes a large towel, a hairdrier and an indelible marker pen. He goes back into the bathroom. He kneels down by the bath. He spreads the towel out on the floor. He takes the corpse out of the water. He wraps it in the towel and pats it down from head to foot. He turns the body over and repeats the operation on its back. He drains the water and carefully rinses the ceramic bath with the shower head. He picks up the scissors, cuts the little girl's fingernails and throws them into the toilet bowl following the same procedure he used for his own. He plugs in the hairdrier. He dries the little girl and sprinkles her with talcum powder, leaving only a small area uncovered, an oval, on her chest. He uncaps the marker pen and there, partly in block letters and partly not, he writes a name.

3

Straddling her client, Celeste hits her head against the roof of the car a third time.

'Gently, you fucker!' She props her hands on his shoulders, showing him that she would need to move only slightly to make him pop out. Then she looks at him severely.

'Sorry,' he whispers, entirely at her mercy. Then he waits for her to continue. And she does continue, eyes closed, writhing and whimpering without ever opening her mouth, as though loving every minute of it. There's no way of knowing if she really is.

The client grips her by the waist, watching her strange dance, his mouth moist, his face frozen in astonishment.

Celeste doesn't open her eyes, but smiles as though she knows, like she's watching him as he finishes himself off between her legs. And that awareness gratifies her, fortifies her. It's nice to think that the man will go home with a fissure in his life.

She ruffles the little hair he has left, and kisses him. The punter opens his eyes wide in wonder as the young girl's tongue wraps itself around his, teases it, explores and rolls it around with passionate hunger.

Celeste does the kissing. It feels right to her, refusing

to let his tongue into her mouth.

The punter tells her he's about to come.

'I know,' says Celeste.

'What about you?' he says.

'Don't you fret,' says Celeste. (Nice, she thinks.)

The man ejaculates, shaken by an orgasm so intense it almost hurts. He smiles at Celeste, who studies the tremors of his body with a sexy pout, and he still can't believe that this ordinary young girl, without lipstick or lipgloss or heels or fishnets, without any of the whorish trappings, this female, not even all that pretty, wearing ordinary clothes, who could have come straight from school, that this girl has just given him, in return for an insignificant share of the contents of his wallet, what he would not have the slightest hesitation in calling the best fuck of his fifty-eight years. He keeps himself inside her to prolong for as long as possible the undeserved pleasure that is already abandoning his body, and runs his hands up and down her back, seeking the bare skin beneath her sweater.

Celeste lets him do that for a while, struck by his gratitude. She listens to his breathing, slightly choked with emotion, strokes his hair and rests her hand on the back of his neck. Then, with one final generous impulse, she squeezes herself as hard as she can against his exhausted member, holding in the last of his erection.

He hugs her, genuinely.

He seeks her mouth to kiss her again. Celeste turns her head to declare the encounter at an end.

She rises off him, her right leg still wrapped in her

jeans, which she had only half taken off (that's young people for you, he thinks in that tiny instant of time: that skilled sloppiness they have, a natural ability to negotiate obstacles without removing them, even incorporating them into their everyday habits), sits down again at a slight angle, slips her other leg into her jeans and pulls them up firmly, arching herself on the seat with a swift and unconsciously suggestive thrust of the pelvis. The punter looks at her, stunned once more.

The rain becomes scattered, subsides and then resumes, hammering violently against the car windows, blown like hail.

'You know I could be your father,' he says, looking her up and down, driven by a sudden impulse of contempt.

Celeste doesn't even turn around. Her mouth reveals the condescension of someone who has heard the same phrase a thousand times.

'Of course I know. And what about you? Do you know?'

The client says nothing. Celeste could swear she hears the sound of guilt.

'You're right, I'm sorry.'

Finally she looks at him. She doesn't open her mouth, but the syntax of that silence is printed between them like a caption.

4

After practising for a while in the corridor, getting his balance right, the man leaves the flat carrying the child on his back in a large, smart rucksack. Contrary to what he expected of the posture he would have to assume, bent forwards is worse. It's as though, after an improbable initial lightness, the corpse is trying to lash out uncontrollably to one side, and someone is restraining it. The best way is straight-backed, as on a military parade. Less clumsy, and less guilty-looking, too.

Clean from head to toe, dark glasses, short trousers, shoes with worn-out soles, windbreaker to hide his perspiration, the man walks down the stairs.

The front door is wide open to catch the early morning air. The man stops by the porter's window. The porter doesn't see him, but greets him anyway, addressing him by name. He goes out into the street, clutching the straps of the rucksack and adopting the light step he practised in the corridor of his flat. It's simpler and less ungainly in a more open space.

To reach the beach he has to cross two minor roads and a major one. It isn't far, but he has to be careful. He's worried about doing something clumsy, committing some unforeseen error. His main concern is rigor mortis. That the packing tape with which he parcelled up the little girl to make her take up as little space as possible might split. And however cinematic the image, he can't shake off the possibility of an arm suddenly popping out of the rucksack, or it developing a telling bulge just as he walks in front of a police car.

And then there's the main road. Crossing it is a fear that he's had since childhood. A wide road that takes a while to get across, where the cars don't give a toss about the pedestrians, and you could find yourself having to jump out of the way at any moment. One March evening, when he was a young boy, he was seized by a fear of falling right in the middle the road. A sudden conviction that he was walking on a gangway, empty space all around him. Strong enough to make him crouch down and continue on all fours to reach the other side. And then there was that intermittent impulse to come to a halt, while the cars hooted like crazy. That dark desire to wait.

He remembers a voice, a sound within him, somehow slowly telling him something about himself. That voice turns gently in his mind, some evenings he comes home and as he climbs the stairs he feels as though he is in the presence of a person he knows, and he sees a scene, a photograph slightly veiled in light. It's cold, it's night-time, it's raining or has just rained, there's an old tiled staircase with a porter's office on the ground floor and inside it a child with the face of an old man who is talking to somebody, but the moment it sees him it breaks off and says: You've come back, you know where your place is, points to the stairs and he looks, there's moss on them, a sickly, rotten smell, go on, the porter repeats the words and he sets off, climbing the slippery steps, as he goes up the smell gets worse and finally he recognises it, he knows what awaits him, he must lie down in the earth with the others, then he quickens his step takes the stairs three at a time opens the door to the flat, sweat drips down his forehead, he's cold, he goes in, locks the door puts it on the latch sits down and breathes, breathes.

Then run. Run the way you've learned. Concentrate on the distraction. Don't think. Nothing will happen. Add up the stretches of road separating you from the beach. It isn't difficult. You've done it before, you can do it again. Run between the people coming towards you, some of them even crash straight into you without noticing. Run beside the queue of cars, the shops that are just opening, the children going to school in groups of two and three. Other people's lives are like an animal that doesn't eat much, merely grown fat from dragging itself along, turning round on itself in endless repetition.

A little further on, a young policeman with a moustache is waving his arms about in a square full of cars. He paces restlessly back and forth, as though he's fighting over something. He shouts, warns, points, puts everything into it but he's surrounded, there are too many of them, he permits and prohibits to an equal extent. His forehead is drenched and he furiously licks at his moustache.

The man heads towards him. He knows he shouldn't,

there's no time, he's taking a pointless risk, and yet he walks straight towards him like he has something important to tell him. He slips between the stationary cars and stops in front of the policeman, panting from the effort of running.

'Can I help you?' asks the policeman, expecting a request for directions. And almost at the same time he puts his whistle to his mouth, preparing to stop a Passat that is trying to ignore an amber light.

The man doesn't speak, but continues jogging on the spot.

The policeman lets his whistle drop back down against his uniform jacket and looks at him with a mixture of suspicion and curiosity. The Passat immediately takes advantage of this.

'What can I do for you?' he says as if repeating himself, enunciating each word very clearly. His tone is no longer polite, and he is already playing a part again.

'My misery haunts me even in my dreams,' the man says, stepping back with the modesty of a teenager being asked out on a first date.

The policeman arches an eyebrow. He looks the man up and down, then down and up, as though following some classificatory procedure. Then he slices the air with his hand, an inch from the man's face.

'Go on, clear off.'

The man stares at him from behind his glasses.

'Some people,' the policeman says right into his face, as if he wasn't there.

Visibly injured by the remark, the man lowers his gaze,

then stares at the policeman (so intensely that the latter can identify the colour of his eyes behind the darkened lenses) and, barely parting his lips, he speaks to him one last time: 'As you wish.'

The policeman looks at him with utter contempt as the man turns his back and continues on his way.

Then the light turns green, and the traffic sucks him back into its vain and constant protest.

Attention: please go back and deposit any metal objects in the appropriate drawer.

Inside the security cabin, a middle-aged man, remarkably reminiscent of a penguin, moves back and forth like a caged beast. He snorts, takes his mobile phone out of his inside jacket pocket and taps the floor with the tip of his shoe as he waits for the doors to open and let him back in.

Celeste, queuing behind him, waits.

The penguin leaves, yelling abuse at the recorded voice, and observes the people queuing with an expression caught halfway between embarrassment and a plea for sympathy.

Celeste enters at her turn, as the man slips his mobile phone into the metal drawer. Once inside, she goes to the waiting-room ticket machine.

The penguin arrives soon after her, studies the room, does a quick headcount of the people ahead of him, looks wearily at Celeste and then proceeds to make a neurotic display of himself, parading along the counters and muttering about being an exploited taxpayer.

Celeste lets him march back and forth a few times and

then, when he passes in front of her again, she gets up and walks over to him, showing him two little numbered tickets.

'Have this,' she says. And she hands him the ticket with the lower number.

The penguin's face suddenly assumes the expression of a twelve-year-old child. He tries to stammer something as he stares disbelievingly at the ticket in his hand.

Celeste goes to her seat, crosses her legs and waits for her turn once more.

A little while later, she's sitting on the other side of a clerk's desk.

'Are your parents account holders?'

'What are account holders?'

'I imagine you have parents.'

'Yeah, and?'

'Do they have an account with us?'

'No.'

The bank clerk puts his fingertips together, brings them to his lips and, leaning forwards, places his elbows delicately on the desk.

'How much did you wish to deposit?'

'Twenty-thousand euros.'

'Twenty-thousand euros. And who would have given you twenty-thousand euros?'

Without making too much of a show, Celeste slips a hand into the back pocket of her trousers and takes out a yellow envelope folded in two and wrapped in an elastic band. She opens it and drops a pile of notes onto the desk, which start to spread like a kind of crab.

The bank clerk glances in all directions, then he looks at her.

'Do you have an older sister, or an adult you trust?'

As she leaves, Celeste's eyes meet those of the penguin, who is filling in a paying-in slip, his dumb expression still fresh on his face.

She walks straight on until she reaches the kerb. She looks at the horizon through the trees of the Villa Comunale, beyond the traffic.

The sea front's so beautiful now.

She waits for the green light, and slowly crosses the road, past the unmoving cars. Then she strolls along the low wall that runs by the sea.

For some reason, when she sees the man with the rucksack sitting among the boats on the beach, she has a sense that something doesn't quite add up.

'My question was: *objective condition of criminal liability*.'

The candidate, bent so far forward that he can't even touch the arms of his chair, twists nervously at his ring finger with its gleaming gold band. Behind him, in the front row, a visibly anxious young woman follows the examination, pretending to ignore the cries of her baby daughter outside the open door of the hall, where she is being lovingly tended by an elderly couple all dressed up for the occasion.

'Criminal liability presupposes that the perpetrator is capable of comprehending and desiring, at the time of the commission of the crime—'

'My question was: *objective condition of criminal liability*.'

There is a mysterious interruption of proceedings in the hall, uniting everyone present in an awkward silence. Some are amused, some indignant; but no one speaks.

The candidate brings his thumb and forefinger to his forehead and glues his eyes to the floor with an expression of resigned suffering, just as a climber, pulling his hands away from the rock, might accept that relinquishing a painful hold will also mean plummeting down to earth.

The minutes that follow expand unbearably until,

from the far side of the desk, the criminal lawyer intervenes. His calm voice seems clearly judged to be a slap in the face:

'Tell us, Dr Vignarelli, is this a state examination or a police interrogation?'

'Excuse me?'

The sense of relief that fills the hall is so vivid you can smell it. Many of the onlookers shift in their seats, greedily enjoying their good fortune at being in the front row to witness the clash. The heads of the members of the commission turn towards the lawyer Heller, who doesn't appear to be terribly interested in his moment of notoriety. The candidate regains possession of the arms of his chair. This detail does not escape the examining magistrate, who is by now almost grinding his teeth.

'Do you want me to repeat my question?' says the lawyer, without modifying his earlier tone or deigning to glance at the magistrate. 'Is this a state exam or a police interrogation?'

The examining magistrate sits back in his chair and glances at the members of the commission sitting on either side of him, already attempting to enlist their support.

'Avvocato Heller, I would be obliged if you would cease interfering with my way of conducting this exam, or at least spare me your observations. I asked only a simple question, I have done so at least three times and I have still not obtained an answer, perhaps you did not hear—'

'Then change the question and have done with this

inquisition. The candidate is here to sit an exam, not to face an indictment.'

The public can barely restrain their applause.

'This is too much. Mr Chairman, please intervene,' the magistrate explodes, suddenly tightening his lips, his face flushed to the eyebrows with a blaze of repressed fury.

'Yes, that does seem like a good idea,' the lawyer concludes with dignified relief. 'Intervene, Mr Chairman, and inform the magistrate where we are, what we are doing and the way in which we are requested to do it.'

The chairman breaks the silence that follows, making a visible effort to choose one side, the only one possible.

'Change the question, Dr Vignarelli.'

Twenty minutes later, the candidate passes his exam.

The subsequent examinations follow mechanically, one after the other, with the melancholy indolence that follows a moment of conflict, when each act becomes entirely routine and the original cause of contention seems less significant than the trouble it created. The questions become simplified to the point of indifference, outlandish concepts go unchallenged, silences and omissions are condoned, as though the incident that has just taken place has lowered the motivation of the entire commission, which is now unexpectedly inclined to extend its benevolence to all and sundry.

Heller asks few questions, tempers imprecise answers, channels the candidates in the right direction and moves on. Vignarelli broadens the scope of his questions and lets errors pass with a deliberate show of nonchalance, acting out a form of civic resentment that points the finger at the institution itself, along the lines of: If you want me to pass know-nothings then fine, I will, let selection and merit go hang, but remember that it's your fault, I have done the best I can. And he underscores this attitude with a series of expressive gestures that might very well have been scripted: contemplating the plasterwork on the ceiling, moving his lips and saying nothing, but producing a faint and intent background noise, folding his arms, releasing them and folding them again. In response Heller opens his eyes wide, staring into the middle distance as though he has just heard a solecism, displaying the concerned compassion of someone who would like to prevent some poor wretch from making a fool of himself but is powerless to do so. And so, among the onlookers, you might observe an expression that absorbs his irony and reflects it back as admiration, and in such moments the young woman magistrate beside him turns and looks at him.

She has noticed him several times in court, she has observed that he is distinguished by his confidence, very different from his colleagues who are always just a little over the top, wrapped up in their gowns and wearing forced expressions, with their baroque vocabulary and rhetorical devices, their servile manners and their lack of any real respect for anybody. This young lawyer is so very different from the others. His total lack of pushiness. The measured way in which he crystallises ideas into a few well-chosen words. His ability to stand inches from the fray without getting involved, allowing others to have their say so that he can then use their own arguments against them and thereby win the case. Socks that always match his pale ties. That slim body on which jackets ripple like snakes. That body which, one morning two months before, she realised she wanted to wrap her arms around even when she wasn't looking at him, when she suddenly became aware of its presence, in a courtroom in which an injury case was being heard. And he hadn't been doing anything special, he hadn't been moving in any of the ways she imagined she liked, how strange, she had thought, as an ancient heat had gripped her belly like hunger, a need to swallow some of that body, to bite it, to find out if its flavour, which all of a sudden she so wanted to experience, was really what had made her mouth water, how strange that all the men I've had are always so different from the way I imagined them, so desires don't mean, they aren't, what's the point of them if things always turn out differently, do I really like this man or do I no longer know what I want, that was what she thought on that white January morning, one of those mornings when the air smells of laundry, all these thoughts had passed through her mind as she sat in court and realised that the man she was now ashamed to look at could influence her life, could make her take decisions, could push her in one direction or another, change her friends and habits, he had all that power and he didn't even know it, but wait a moment, she had thought again, I'm in this room with him, I've discovered that he exists, David Heller is his name,

Avvocato David Heller (how full that name is now, how
substantial; how different his ordinary profession seems
to me now, how well it suits him), and he doesn't know
about me, he doesn't know the secret I carry inside me,
a secret about him, and who knows how long I've been
brooding on this and only now has it appeared, she could
almost see herself sitting there on the worn-out padding
of a nasty antique armchair, in that absurd situation, just
look at what's happening to you, falling in love (falling
in love? what was she thinking about?) during a trial,
with a poor wretch handcuffed in a cage a few metres
away from her, waiting for a decision about his freedom,
a decision that depended on words and precise
distinctions while her body was filled with that sense of
expectation, already impatient even if she didn't know
where to start, if she too had been a lawyer how many
opportunities she would have had to get close to him, to
make him notice her, but as things were, with him
coming and going, silent and reserved, never giving
himself away, her only hope was for a courtroom
association, the two of them together on the same case
even if on opposite sides, one day he would knock at the
door of her office and, standing in the doorway, he
would say: Excuse me, I'm Heller, the defence lawyer of
. . . and she sitting at her desk would lift her eyes from
the papers she was examining and as she turned towards
him her expression would change from concentration to
shy surprise, and warmed by the sun on her back falling
through the window, she would say only: Yes, and he, so
moved by her beauty that words failed him, would say: I

wanted to ask . . . I'm sorry, that is, I know we're in preliminary investigation but could you just tell me if . . . and from that moment they would have many more opportunities to meet and she would surely conquer him sooner or later, but if all those things really did happen, and if the situation did play out so perfectly according to plan, and if in the meantime he found someone else, if he already had someone else, please, no, let it not be so . . . these were the thoughts of magistrate Elena Cassinari when she discovered the existence of David Heller and while, out of an instinctive need to classify, she raced after all the fragments of her emotions like a cat after her kittens, to bring them back and reassemble what was happening to her so as to give it some kind of order and even a name, inside her she felt something pulsing, an unknown quantity of different desires that unsettled her and at the same time relieved her of her everyday concerns which now seemed cheap and pointless, and then with a great effort she looked straight at him and when finally for one dense, clotted moment, she met his surprised and vaguely comprehending eyes, she felt a sense of relief, a parting of the clouds, she knew that one day she would summon up the courage to tell him, of this, yes, she was utterly convinced, it was something she had to do.

And in fact some time later, perhaps a week, when she met him outside the court library and greeted him, he was kind and helpful and from that point they became friends. Sometimes she asks him if he is busy after the hearings, and every now and again he waits for her and they go to a little bar nearby, they have an aperitif or if they have to go back to court they have something to eat and share a carafe of white wine, he always pays and she knows that he has finally worked it out.

And now the exam session is over and she's impatient to leave because he's waiting for her outside, he's accepted a lift from her, and they might even stop for a drink before going home, she can't wait to join him but a member of the commission keeps her back, nothing important, ordinary small talk, the legal niceties required of her in such situations, and as she dutifully replies, as though this chit-chat meant something to her, she is counting one by one the seconds that are being taken away from her.

The little crowd of candidates and relatives stands around chatting happily at the entrance to the building. They are going through the sequence of questions from the exam in detail, as though by working through the memories they might keep them from floating away, confirming everything that has happened and thus obtaining some kind of consolation. Someone's uncle takes a bottle and some plastic cups from a bag, pulls out the cork and distributes the wine indiscriminately.

Standing by the exit, Heller waits for the friend who has offered to join him. With his attention fixed momentarily on the voices of the crowd, he doesn't notice the young woman who first looks at him insistently, then overcomes the embarrassment that holds her back and walks towards him.

'Excuse me, please,' he hears, before turning towards the unfamiliar voice.

The woman addressing him is young, almost as tall as he is, dressed carefully and rather formally.

'Have we met?' he asks.

'My name is Venturi,' she says, gesturing with a barely perceptible nod to someone behind her, a short distance away. 'I felt I ought to thank you.'

Heller looks past the woman to a little girl in the arms of the candidate he had defended shortly before, during the exam. Instantly a thought takes shape, before fading away again: women have a remarkable way of using space to declare their affiliations.

'Oh. My pleasure,' he says, narrowing his eyes slightly.

'If it hadn't been for you they'd have failed him.'

'Perhaps. But I think he did well.'

The woman comes closer, staring at him with complicity, making clear to him that she appreciates his elegance. She keeps her eyes on him for a moment too long, before retreating as though acting out an ambivalent desire.

Heller would happily have watched as she walked away, but for Dr Vignarelli's sudden, grim-faced appearance.

'My compliments, Avvocato Heller, sincerely. A fine presentation.'

Heller doesn't immediately reply, and when he does, it is in an unmistakeably patronising tone.

'Nothing personal, Dr Vignarelli. I just saw a candidate in difficulties and kept him from being failed.'

'And are you sure I would have failed him?'

'Absolutely.'

His teeth gritted, the magistrate exhales noisily, and as that tiny piece of life departs it releases tension from his features, revealing a wounded innocence that doesn't escape Heller's notice. In some ways, he thinks, this man is sincere. My response was an assault on Vignarelli's moral code, a possession to which he has devoted a considerable part of his life and which he jealously protects against assault. And the simple fact that just such an assault has occurred calls for a reaction on his part, and that reaction is, for the time being, nothing but bluster and flushed alarm. Here he is, seized by this impotent rage that he is unable to channel or direct, as though trying to produce a sound that refuses to come.

Heller perceives all this in an instant. He's so convinced of it that he would be willing to sign an affidavit. But some impulse drives him in the other direction: in fact, the discovery of this unexpected weakness in Vignarelli makes him lash out even more savagely.

'You are a presumptuous man, Heller,' the magistrate finally manages to say. 'First you wanted to call me arrogant and I allowed you to do so, but in fact it is you who are arrogant. You have had your fun, riding roughshod over me in front of the commission and the public, slighting both me and my function. You should be ashamed of yourself.'

'No, you're wrong. There's nothing personal to it, I told you that.'

'Oh, but there is, there most certainly is. And I want to tell you another thing: you're so keen on defending criminals that you've lost all respect for the institution of the law.'

'On the contrary, you're so used to prosecuting criminals that you treat everyone as if they're guilty.'

Visibly surprised by Heller's response, the magistrate takes the blow, and raises his eyebrows, unable to conceal his admiration.

Heller could take advantage of this pause to lay into his adversary, with a hint of a smile, or else simply allow the point he has scored to curdle between them into a crudely meaningful silence. But he does nothing of the sort. He looks away, wondering why his lady friend is taking so long.

And he has already braced himself when Vignarelli, lips trembling, approaches him as though to examine the label of his tie, and whispers in his ear: 'The world of the law is a small one, if you catch my drift. Or to put it rather more bluntly, you'll pay for this, you bastard.'

And the magistrate walks off, smiling, to suggest to any onlookers that he was merely passing on a piece of gossip, an amusing anecdote, thus creating an impression of intimacy and confidentiality which played down the preceding outburst, as if coming to blows and then acting as though nothing had happened was an essential part of relations between such people as themselves.

Heller lets him do this, without losing his composure. There is, in his passivity, a kind of pre-emptive awareness of Vignarelli's strategy, and the magistrate may well be conscious of this as he turns his back on Heller and walks away.

People begin to emerge from the court. In a brief moment of confusion, Heller's gaze falls on the face of a woman he knows. It settles there for a moment longer than necessary, long enough for her eyes to give an unmistakeable flash of recognition. Then, with a nod of his head, he beckons to her.

Immediately she comes over.

'Magistrato!' Heller calls to the group of examiners pausing on the steps of the hall.

Vignarelli turns abruptly, surprised at the lawyer's voice and its unexpected warmth.

'Please excuse me,' says Heller, approaching him with the attitude of someone who doesn't wish to disturb. And he places himself between the magistrate and the woman, spreading his arms towards her. 'I wanted to introduce you to this lady.'

He is behaving quite informally, as though introducing Vignarelli to someone the magistrate really ought to meet.

Although still disconcerted by Heller's behaviour, the magistrate allows his manners to prevail, and extends his hand towards the woman.

She shakes it with a smile. The magistrate can't help but notice a curious gleam in her blue eyes.

'Signora Venturi,' says Heller.

Vignarelli looks at him, perplexed. He and the woman are still vaguely shaking hands.

'The wife of the candidate we passed a moment ago,' Heller explains.

The magistrate's indignation seems about to shatter his features. He darts a look at Heller, his eyes full of menace.

'So you're still here? I thought you'd gone already. Oh, good evenin,' says a breathless Elena Cassinari who has suddenly joined them. 'Let's go, or I'll get a ticket.'

'Dr Cassinari,' Vignarelli greets her without taking his eyes off Heller. And before continuing he pauses, a brief and rancorous silence.

'We will meet again, Heller. Don't worry, because whatever happens, we will meet again.'

Frozen with embarrassment, Elena Cassinari listens to her colleague, aware of having arrived at the worst possible moment. The candidate's wife walks away, pleased to have repaid a favour. Heller takes his leave of Vignarelli with a nod, slips his arm into his companion's and walks with her to the exit.

Shortly afterwards they're in her car, in the slowly moving traffic. A light rain is falling.

'What happened with Vignarelli? Did you still have something to discuss?'

'No, it was my fault,' says Heller, shaking his head, and, as though talking to himself, with a sudden feeling of revulsion: 'I should have left things as they were, why, why can't I control myself . . . ?'

'You don't strike me as the kind of person who can't control himself,' she says, lifting and closing her fingers on the steering wheel.

'You don't know me, Elena,' Heller says, turning slightly to face her. 'I like to crush people.'

She turns slowly and looks at him inquiringly.

'Why do you tell me these things?'

'I'm sorry,' Heller replies in an entirely different tone, as though he has just emerged from a momentary trance. 'Just ignore me, I've had a bad day.'

And he stares out of the rain-spattered window, removing himself entirely from the needs of the woman beside him, as a heavy silence fills the car.

He sees himself, sitting on the beach between two fishing boats with girls' names, the sea very close, the city on the other side, humming a pop song as he waits for the right moment.

It all went better than he had expected. He abandoned the rucksack beneath the prow of one of the boats and left, not running now but walking calmly, just as he had decided he would, his sense of confidence growing by the moment, certain that every step away from the beach brought him closer to impunity.

Returning to his building, he greeted the porter, who had set up his little folding chair on the footpath outside. When he addressed the porter loudly by name, the man replied, 'Bless you Mr Heller, you've still got your health and all your marbles.' He spoke with a resigned admiration, seeing the lawyer in his sports clothes yet again, and so early in the day.

Heller went upstairs and quickly washed himself. Invigorated by his run, he came back downstairs wearing a suit and tie, his athletic appearance elegantly heightened by his formal attire. The porter looked at him differently, as one might appraise someone who has recently had a facelift.

And his life began to repeat itself, the same as always.

Until yesterday.

When he opened his mailbox.

He wants to ask the porter if he'd seen anybody putting anything into the slot.

There was no stamp on the envelope.

Inside, cut with scissors, was a piece of the rucksack into which he had stuffed the little girl.

'Fancy a bite to eat before we go home?'

'No thanks, I'm rather tired.'

As she watches Heller get out of the car and walk along the footpath, magistrate Elena Cassinari drives off slowly and considers her new situation.

If she had to use an image to describe it, perhaps a motorcyclist getting to his feet after a bad fall and patting himself all over, his helmet still on his head, and saying: Nothing, it's nothing.

It's nothing.

The tractors

Once they took me to my grandma's and I saw something dying in the grass. A bird, I recognised it from the tremble of its wings, desperate, as though it were trying not to be swallowed up by the earth. Then I saw its claws contracting, pointing upwards. I wasn't far away.

By the time I reached it, it had stopped struggling. I saw its chest swell beneath the feathers. It was panting, but gently, so as not to waste its strength, to stay alive for as long as possible. It was very dirty, I couldn't work out what colour it was. I tried to look at its eyes. That's something one does quite naturally, when trying to help someone who isn't feeling well.

I've never liked birds' eyes. The tiny crescents, nothing but fear and hunger. But these eyes looked at me as though I were a stranger, someone you wouldn't want near you.

I wanted to pick it up in one hand to warm it. But when I went to it, it shivered and kicked, showing its claws. Then I took a step back and let it die as it wanted to.

I don't know how long I stood there. I worked out that it was dead when a little breeze stirred its feathers. They hadn't moved before, or at least not like that. Its eyes were closed now. They had eyelids and veins and wrinkles in the corners, like old people have.

I blew my nose in my fingers, rubbed them on the grass and started digging with my bare hands. I dug till the stones ended and I reached the brown earth. Then I nudged the bird with the back of my hand and let it fall into the hole. When it touched the bottom, its wings looked as though they were trying to escape, its head fell to one side and one eye opened.

I felt a great lump in my throat.

Quickly I threw earth into the hole. Then I levelled it

out with my hands and spread a handful of pebbles on the top so that you couldn't see anything any more.

That evening, at dinner, I asked Grandma if tractors passed that way. She isn't the kind of person who would say, What are you asking me something like that for, as my mother certainly would have. She just said, 'No, there aren't any tractors around here.'

That calmed me and we ate beans on toast, green peppers and, for afters, some custard that Grandma had made specially for me.

Grandma doesn't like you to talk when you're eating. She chews very, very slowly, partly because she hasn't got many teeth, and partly because she just likes it that way. It makes you restless.

Then in the morning I got up with an idea in my head. Grandma's answer wasn't enough. I wanted to ask her another question, but she was still asleep. So I ran to the window. When I saw it was raining I felt better, because when it rains the tractors don't come out, I thought. I went downstairs, to the shed beside the kitchen. I never went in there for fear of rats. But this time I did go in, scraping my feet even though I hadn't trodden in any mud. I remembered seeing some tins, at the bottom of the white cupboard where Grandma kept useful things. They were still there. I took out a metal one, a biscuit tin. It was full of old light bulbs. I wondered what I would tell Grandma if she burst in on me. Then I thought she wouldn't say anything, or at worst, Not that one, take this one here.

By the time I got outside it had stopped raining. There

was a smell of autumn, leaves and damp earth. The trees spread their branches wide. But I was close to tears.

It wasn't easy to find the hole, I'd done a good job the day before. I put the tin down on the ground and started digging with my hands again. I put the earth I removed into the tin. When the grey of the bird began to appear I enlarged the hole and went on digging all round it, so as to roll it out without having to see or touch it. Then I put it in the tin and went back inside. Meanwhile Grandma had got up, I could hear her footsteps upstairs. She didn't call me.

I hid the tin in the fireplace and went up to see her. Then we went into the vegetable garden and I helped her. She explained things to me as she did them. I felt like a thief.

'Grandma,' I said, 'I took one of your tins while you were asleep.'

'What tin?' she asked.

'A metal one, with light bulbs in.'

'And what did you want with that?'

'I didn't want to leave a dead bird in the ground.'

'Hence the tractors,' she said, more to herself than in response to me.

'Yes,' I admitted.

When we got back, Grandma asked me to give her the tin. She took one of her plants, pulled it out of its pot, threw the earth away and replaced it with the soil from the tin.

In the evening my parents came to get me.

I'd always liked going to Grandma's. There was a

whole ritual whenever I arrived. First there were the old tiles outside the house. They were organised by colour, white, orange. A few blue ones. Grandma had arranged them very nicely.

A hop, like that, from one row to the next, on one foot.

Then the apple tree. Foot on the bump at the bottom, it looks like a step, as though it were there on purpose. A tiny jump and you're hanging from the biggest branch. A big push and you can get your elbows on it.

Then a tour of the whole of the outside of the house, my inspection; then finally I went in. Grandma's smell everywhere. In the dining-room table drawer there was an exercise book held together by an elastic band. I didn't read it, I didn't even open it, the important thing was that it was still there. I just ran a finger over the cover.

I climbed onto a chair to reach the tall cupboard with the cups inside. I opened and touched them. I had to touch things one by one, like a blind girl.

Every now and again, distractedly, I would glance at that plant.

7

Celeste, her nostrils still full of the smell of talcum powder, her hands under the tap, rubs her thumb and fingertips together to make the universal gesture for money. She can still feel the roughness of the glue. To get rid of the glue under her fingernails all she had to do was cut them; but she only seems to be moving the glue on her skin from one place to another rather than rubbing it off.

She repeats the operation a number of times, drying her fingers one by one, but when she clenches her fists and opens them again, she can still feel the stickiness. She draws one hand close to her face, turns it round and holds it out, studying it from every angle for any last remaining traces. Then, with a gesture that smacks curiously of repression, she rubs her hands together and waves them in the air, averting her head as if to avoid being blinded by a powder that she has never actually touched.

All of a sudden she emerges, irritably, from the bathroom. She almost collides with her mother, about to knock on the door to tell her that dinner is ready. Celeste lowers her eyes, visibly uneasy at being surprised in the middle of a sulk that she couldn't explain even if she wanted to. Her mother looks into the bathroom behind her daughter, as though she might find the reason for her mood somewhere there.

'I'm coming,' says Celeste, and walks ahead of her along the corridor.

'Have you been using talcum powder?' her mother asks her.

Celeste turns. She hadn't thought of this.

'What?'

'Talcum powder, I said,' her mother replies, tapping her nose with the tip of her index finger. 'I can smell it.'

'Oh, yeah,' replies Celeste, trying to avoid her mother's eye.

With his unbuttoned shirt revealing his frail chest, Celeste's father chews slowly as he patiently watches a mattress salesman on TV. As Celeste walks past him, she strokes the back of his hand, the one holding a spoon. He lifts his head and glances at her as you might glance at a passenger who has just entered your train compartment.

Celeste sits down.

'I've made some soup, do you want some?' her mother asks as she enters.

'Hey, why not,' Celeste replies, looking at her father, who resumes his chewing, his eyes fixed on the shopping channel presenter who is now approaching the camera to tell her father how far he would rise in his estimation if he would only pick up the phone.

Celeste admires the beauty of the man responsible for her existence. She appreciates his slim frame, the symmetry of his wrinkles, his slow manner; even the symptoms of the illness that has been sapping his attention and his memory for nearly two years. There was always a natural finesse about his movements, a natural respect for other people's space. The kind of person who would always wait and let you finish whatever you were doing before doing anything himself.

What has he been thinking about all day? Celeste wonders, looking at him tenderly. What does he see when he sits down by the window after lunch? How does he feel in that body as it imposes its needs upon him? Does he even remember that he has a daughter?

Sometimes he addresses her as though he recognises her, as if contact between them had never been interrupted, as he used to speak to her before the day when he got up, crossed the flat, poking his head into room after room with the delicacy of a guest and Celeste, who was in the kitchen getting something from the fridge, heard him come in and had said, There's some hot coffee left if you want some, and he had replied, Don't worry, and Celeste, turning around, had immediately understood that the body in front of her no longer contained her father, and had stared for a long time at his pyjamas, his striped pyjamas with the buttons that now seemed so different from those she had seen him wearing thousands of times, they looked like someone else's pyjamas, a prisoner's, perhaps, or an old man's: loose, slack, and dirtier than she remembered.

Since that day life has been nothing but a matter of waiting and time suspended, she's established an unspoken agreement with her mother that they will continue to behave as they always have and that everything in the house will remain exactly where it had been.

Most importantly, Celeste has never believed that his condition is permanent, and when all of a sudden he speaks to her, calling her by name, she pretends not to feel the lump that comes into her throat and replies without surprise, without condescension, exactly as he would want. Every day she tells herself that it will pass, that just as they lost him one morning, one morning they will find him again, they just have to wait.

'You know we've dealt with the heating today?' says her mother enthusiastically, talking to Celeste but turning to face her husband.

Celeste looks up from her plate.

'So we don't even have to have the man in,' her mother goes on, raising her voice slightly, the tone of someone who wasn't heard the first time. Then she pours herself a bowl of soup and sits down. Celeste loosens and tightens her fingers on the handle of the spoon. She can still feel the stickiness.

'What happened?' she asks.

'A stupid thing,' her mother says, looking at her husband, who doesn't join in. 'Paolo remembered. You know the little white dial under the boiler, the one furthest away from the wall? You just have to move that. The water-level indicator had dropped below zero, can you imagine?'

'That was why it was cutting out every couple of days,'

Celeste explains needlessly, directing her words to her father.

'Only 520,' says the man on the television. 'We're practically giving them away.'

'Do you remember?' her mother asks after a short but painful silence.

Celeste says no. And she remembers the expression on the little girl's face when she took the sticky tape off her mouth. She looked disappointed, she thinks.

'Paolo worked it out straight away. He heard me complaining about the cold water, he went to the boiler, put his hand in underneath and corrected it as if he'd done the same thing only the other day,' her mother concludes in the tender expectation of a reply from her husband, which isn't forthcoming. Then she stirs the soup with her spoon, brings it to her mouth and gulps down her mortified hope.

Celeste can just about bring herself to look at her mother, the failure etched on her mouth is so painful. She would rather have a fresh pain than those little joys denied. She would prefer genuine, proper suffering to the wretchedness of happiness that refuses to come. She finishes her soup, drinks half a glass of water and sets down her spoon, taking it from one hand with the other.

As she gets to her feet she senses that her mother has noticed the strange way she was holding her cutlery. Instinctively she hurries out, as though fearing a request for explanations.

'Going already?' she hears from behind her as she

reaches the door.

She's about to turn around, but then changes her mind.

Once she has reached her bedroom she shuts the door, switches on the overhead light and then that on the chest of drawers, which she half covers with an open book. She turns off the overhead light. She lies down on the bed, pushes off her shoes with her toes and lets them fall on the floor. She undresses without getting up. She folds her clothes and presses them to her belly like a cuddly toy. Against her eyelids she sees flashes and streams of light, the day's closing credits. More recent memories tug at her from all sides, each clamouring for its place ahead of all the others. And rebelling against her mind's attempts to devote a part of itself to each, the memories begin to jostle one another, and after a while they clash, hurt themselves and scatter. Some of them die, and some retain some life.

Celeste abandons herself to viewing these mutilated scenes, and in a minute she's somewhere else.

A boy is breathing rhythmically in one of her ears, lying against her back.

She doesn't like the way he's touching her.

She twists an arm behind her and presses a hand against his chest. That little bit of leverage is enough to push him away.

She slips into her jeans, and starts to get out of the car.

Again, Celeste thinks.

She doesn't look at him.

He leaves her be, for now.

The roar of a passing plane, and the scene changes. Someone is knocking on the door. Celeste recognises the shock of blonde hair and the black overalls behind the frosted glass. She's at school.

'Excuse me, Miss, class is over,' says the cleaning lady as she opens the door, as though repeating a phrase by rote.

The teacher, her words still suspended in the air above the class, turns round: 'When on earth are they going to fix that bloody bell,' she says impatiently.

Then a second's pause. 'No, I'm not cross with you. In fact I'm sorry that you have to act as a living bell. As if we didn't all have enough work to do already.'

The cleaner, not taken in for a moment by the woman's tone, puts her head to one side and raises her eyebrows until her forehead is a mass of wrinkles, with the air of someone looking over their shoulder, convinced they have seen something. Then, with an exaggeratedly false smile, she taps her fingers on the door handle, as though accusing the teacher of hypocrisy.

Celeste and her classmates look at one another, caught between laughter and embarrassment.

The cleaning woman lingers in the doorway for a few seconds to work the silence, the teacher looking at her as though unable to understand her manner. Then she turns on her heel and goes, leaving the door wide open.

Just look at her.

Celeste gets up from her desk, walks to the window, climbs onto the sill without alarming any of her classmates in the slightest, says goodbye and climbs down a ladder placed there for that very purpose.

In her memory, as soon as she sets her foot on the ground school has disappeared, and so has her desk, and she's already on the coast road. She walks very close to the low wall, adjusting her pace to echo that of the man in the hooded sweatshirt. She isn't worried that he might notice her, he seems to be concentrating so hard on getting away from the beach. The rucksack's still under the boat. She's sure she'll find it if she hurries.

From a short distance she watches the man crossing the road. Strange, he seems to be frightened of the cars.

She waits for him to reach at least halfway, before crossing the street herself at the same green light. A little boy waves from a stationary tram. Celeste waves back cheerily, as though she recognises him.

By the time she gets to the other side the man has disappeared. Idiot, she says to herself. And she looks all around her for a few seconds, senselessly indicating the cardinal points with her head. She decides to focus on the direction towards which the man seemed to be headed a moment before.

And then she sees him again. It seems so obvious now. He took one of the little alleyways that lead to the old part of the city. Even from a distance Celeste guesses that he has slowed his pace, and immediately interprets this as a sign of increased self-confidence.

She hurries to catch up with him, and when she has gained some ground she slows down, trying to move much more carefully than she did on the coast road, as though filled by a sudden fear that she might be spotted, a fear that she immediately takes seriously. And the more she follows him the more this impression is reinforced.

The man walks with growing assurance, stopping now and again to adjust his hair, his socks or his sunglasses. Celeste crosses the road, varying her distance until she sees her quarry stop by a door and approach a middle-aged man sitting on a folding chair beneath the entryphone. Then she crosses the road, and walks past as the man in the chair hails the other man loudly.

Hey, what a weird surname.

Again, the click of a door handle. Another door opening. But a real one this time; and she's inside. She realises this precisely when, opening her eyes, she feels like she has fallen asleep and woken up at exactly the same time.

Her mother has come in, doing her best not to make any noise, but the presence in the room is unmistakeably hers. Celeste recognises her by her embarrassment, the hesitancy of her movements, the lovely feeling she gets from being seen in that defenceless position, her clothes hugged to her body, on the same bed she has slept in since she was a little girl. Even in the darkness, even in her disoriented state, even with her eyes closed, her mother emanates the indefinable jumble of family qualities that she has always had within herself, and which she would able to identify whatever the lighting. She is almost moved to reflect that a person might be summed up by those qualities. And she pretends to be asleep, partly out of respect for her mother, and partly because she knows the reason for her intrusion.

Her mother comes over to her. Celeste, all her senses alerted by her mother's presence, senses the weight of her eyes on her lips, her neck, her arms, her hands. Then the inspection comes to an end, and she feels the clothes she was holding slip away as though taken by the fingers of a novice thief. Then she sees her mother holding out the collar of her shirt and studying it at an angle, as she might if she wasn't entirely convinced that she had ironed something properly.

Only then does she turn onto her side, making the springs of the mattress creak slightly. She inhales deeply, to lend a regular cadence to her sleepy breathing. Enough to make her mother lay her clothes over the back of the chair at her desk and creep from the room for fear of discovery.

8

Sitting at the desk in his study, David Heller is reading the forensic report from a murder trial. The victim was killed by a shot fired a short distance away from his face. The rifle was loaded with a Brenneke bullet of the kind customarily used for big-game hunting.

The doctor's syntax is intriguingly dry. It describes, second by second, the devastating trajectory of the projectile through the body whose life it has destroyed, it confidently pronounces the complicated names of the organs struck, outlining the traumas and the chain of reactions, it estimates the precise moments at which the damage occurred and the forms it took, then delineates the final exit with the cold detachment of the medical profession.

This language is free of pain. In fact it contains a veiled respect for an enemy who may be difficult to catch, but about whom everything is known.

Science, by reducing life to a system, rapidly generates symptoms of inferiority in the reader. It is these that Heller experiences as he runs his eyes over the concluding lines of the report.

While his chosen profession frequently brings him into close contact with this branch of medicine, each time he encounters its language he becomes aware of a faint sense of obscurantism that impedes the play of his intelligence and puts him in a very particular state of apprehension.

Heller usually reacts to this feeling by going on reading as though nothing was wrong. After a while, though, his eyes freeze on the page.

Still seated, he moves away from the desk, struck by a sudden intuition that powerfully invades his thoughts. He sees it clearly before him, so perfectly composed that he almost wants to write it down.

Science knows only evil. It is evil that makes it prick up its ears.

Prompted by this aphorism, he returns to the case file with a renewed confidence, and thinks once more about the autopsies he saw in the chancellery of the Court of Assizes a few days before. They were arranged in sequence, to enhance the documentation of each individual step of the examination by enlarging the same image from different angles and in ever greater detail. A kind of pornography of death.

The first showed the entire body of the murdered man, lying on the dissecting table. The naked body of an adult male, of medium height, without bruises, without injuries, without blood. And without a face.

The head was there. And the hair. But in the middle, a hole. A crater of exposed flesh. It looked as though the man had been ferociously attacked with an enormous spoon that had removed his features all at once, leaving that horrendous oval as testimony to its passage. A typical spectacle of death by gunshot. A scene of war.

As a general rule, Heller doesn't get so involved in his professional engagements. But never before has he needed to keep his mind so alert.

The defendant, a semi-literate farm labourer in his seventies, was surprised and flattered by the receptiveness shown to him by a lawyer so urbane in his manners, so elegantly dressed and so clearly accustomed to a different class of client. He had placed all his hope in him, immediately offering to sign a mandate and pay him the largest deposit he could manage. Heller refused, insisting that his official engagement paid him well enough. And he threw himself into the case as though he had taken it personally to heart.

He shuts the file, puts his hands in his pockets, goes to the window and looks out. Nothing has happened, and in a sense that worries him.

For two days he has lived between bedroom and study. In the past twenty-four hours he must have paced the flat from end to end at least three times in search of a hair, a fingernail, any trace that the little girl might have left somewhere. He has polished and rubbed and peered and scrubbed inch by inch all the rooms she was allowed to enter. And although he is convinced that he did this as attentively as possible, he is continually seized by the anxiety that one corner or another might have escaped his inspection.

The previous afternoon, out of an unthinking need for activity, he went into the bedroom, opened the wardrobe and stopped to look at his clothes, his hands locked behind his head as though he couldn't remember what he was doing. Then, impulsively, he decided to destroy all the clothes he had worn recently in case they harboured clues. He pulled them out and folded them one at a time. He looked through his carrier bags for the largest, a bag of thick paper with string handles. He doesn't know whether to go through with his decision, but for the time being the bag is there, ready to be eliminated.

At night he thinks. He reconstructs his recent past with chronological precision. Who he has seen, who he has met, whom he has spoken to, and about what. How many faces were imprinted on his mind on the morning when he carried the little girl to the beach. He rebukes himself for having chosen a place so close to home. He has no idea who could have followed him, watched him, or had even the faintest reason for suspecting him. He is convinced that he remained alert at all times, even if the facts throw the grossest of blunders back in his face: an excess of self-confidence, in a word: presumption. Otherwise his life strikes him as unimpeachable, as always. His worries, his movements, his regular haunts and, more generally, his habits are so few and so limited that if there had been a single event worthy of suspicion, he would have identified it straight away.

During the day there are moments when he feels he has nothing to worry about. And he even finds himself wondering whether the scissored scrap of rucksack that he took from his mailbox that morning might not have been a creation of his own guilty mind. But this doubt lasts only for a second. Long enough to open the desk drawer and find it exactly where he put it. Then he picks it up, follows its jagged outlines with his fingers, turns it over and holds it close to his eyes as though imagining that he might be able to find some kind of mark there, a sign, a code that would miraculously lead him to the stranger who has slipped into his life.

That's what he wants. He wants me to wait for him. To know he exists. He's persecuting me with his absence. He has me where he wants me, so that he can turn up whenever he feels like it. When I'm weak enough to comply with all his conditions.

And how will he come? Will he use the phone, email, the post? Or perhaps one morning, sitting on a bench in a café, I'll hear a phrase that will freeze my blood and, turning around, I'll find him in front of me, and he'll smile at me, finally letting me see his face, which I'll have a sense of having seen before, and never knowing when and where, and he'll make a gesture, any kind of gesture, perhaps he'll stir his coffee with a spoon and I will know immediately what his hand looks like and I will feel its grip, and then he will start asking questions, he will speak to me in allusive and circular language and with each phrase I will feel pain, I will struggle not to let panic take hold of me and I will lose all my bearings, I will have to sit down, hold onto something, suppress the rash and senseless drive to attack him physically, and he will notice immediately, I will see his satisfaction as I grow more impotent, he will half close his eyes and give a little smile as though things have gone precisely according to plan, and he will become condescending, he will tell me not to get excited, to remain calm and listen, he will issue his first instructions and when he has finished he will go, my boss now, perhaps even leaving me with his bill to pay, and those few cents that I spend on his behalf will weigh on me like an insult, and soon I will be measuring the length of the leash he has put on me to gauge what freedom of movement I still have and all of a sudden my eye will focus on the normality all around me, I will notice the cut of a raincoat, the colour of a tie, the cellophane of a pack of cigarettes on a table, the clink of a teaspoon in a cup. I will envy the barman who spends his day standing at the espresso machine in exchange for a pathetic wage, I will imagine him getting up at five in the morning, and see him coming out into the street, pulling up the zip of a worn red windcheater and walking in the cold morning, his fists clenched in his pockets all the way to the tram stop, where he will light his first cigarette and have a coughing fit that will give him an imaginary pain in his arm.

What an enviable life you lead, I will think.

Still standing at the window, Heller raises his arms, links his fingers behind his head, smooths back his hair and sighs. Then he returns to his case.

The ring of the telephone takes him by surprise, jerking him upright in his revolving chair. He nearly drops the file. He picks up the receiver, suddenly aware that his legs are trembling.

A woman's voice, a young woman's. Very young.

'Avvocato Heller?'

'Yes, speaking.'

And as he says it he realises he's been caught out once again.

'Good evening, Avvocato, I'm calling from the Vernucchi Company in Tuscany: the land of Chianti and Brunello. I imagine that these are places you are familiar with.'

Heller, who has long experience of telemarketing, receiving between two and four unwanted telesales calls each week from insurance companies, finance firms, carpet salesmen and professional associations that produce pointless magazines, trying to persuade him to subscribe, comes out with a practised phrase before the caller has time to expand on her offer. 'I'm sorry, I don't recognise the name of the law firm. Can you remind me which case we're talking about?'

At the other end of the line the girl falls silent, as though caught out in an oral test at school. It's as though someone has pulled a carpet out from under her feet, and she can't help but fall. A question like that demands a direct answer. And she provides one, putting herself exactly where Heller wants her.

'No, there is no case, our company was just contacting you to—'

'Then you will excuse me, if it isn't work-related I'll have to go,' Heller interrupts, following a pattern he has employed many times in the past.

The girl rallies, still trying to make the best of it. But she knows the situation is all but hopeless. Heller's polite firmness has already defeated her. Previously succinct and enthusiastic, her tone is hesitant now.

'Avvocato, just let me tell you what I'm talking about, and then you'll be entirely free to accept or refuse.'

I wonder, Heller thinks. But he spares her this reflection.

'We're a growing company in the field of wine production. We supply some of the finest hotels and restaurants internationally, but at the moment we're offering the best of our annual production directly to private individuals. So we think that this suggestion might interest—'

At this point Heller interrupts her, throwing his final card onto the table. And it's a trump.

'Please be patient, and I'll try and explain myself a little better. This is a legal practice, and I am at work. The telephone number on which you have called me is a work number. If you call me at this number, which is a work number, for reasons that concern not my work but yours, I have no reason to stay on the line and talk to you.'

'Thank you very much,' the girl says irritably. 'Speak to you soon.'

And there is a tiny pause before she hangs up.

What do you mean, 'Speak to you soon'? Heller thinks with surprise, as he replaces the receiver.

He returns to his case, and opens the file at random. He finds himself reading a copy of one of the police transcripts.

The defendant fired through the grille of his ground-floor window. Before carrying out the killing, he even had a brief conversation with his victim, whom he had surprised and recognised in his garden in the dead of night.

Heller stares at one of the first statements made by the accused, a passage he marked in pencil the first time he read through the file, clearly indicating that it had some significance to which he might usefully return after a more detailed examination of the entire file.

'He said to me: "You don't scare me with your rifle, if I want to get in I'll get in." And from the other side of the bars he grabbed the rifle by the barrel. "You don't know how to shoot, you old dickhead, you're shitting yourself. If I want to get in, I'll get in," he kept repeating. And he said that if I didn't believe him he was about to show me.'

Heller suddenly looks up from the documents, stares into the middle distance and narrows his eyes. He folds his arms, then frees one hand and brings it to his mouth.

He strokes his upper lip with his index finger. Then he nods.

He has to think about it for a little while longer, find some appropriate legal precedent, but he is already sure that he has hit upon a coherent line of defence.

9

'Are you scared of the dog?'

The Great Dane is pretty impressive, the size of a small horse. A male: its testicles, excessively pink, hang arrogantly beneath a tail that periodically whips the air. Its body is statuesque, seemingly disproportionate to its head; its gleaming coat clearly suggests a proper diet. Its back legs are slightly bent. It's a coiled spring waiting to go off.

Celeste, her back pressed against a parked car, tries to move as little as possible. As she attempts to shrink away, her torso bends slightly forwards, perversely drawn by her terror of the creature's jaws.

The dog's back is arched, its intentions ambiguous, either wanting to mount her or wanting to tear her to pieces. Its eyes are inexpressive. From time to time it growls, producing a cavernous rumble. With impatient and irritable darts of its tongue it regularly collects the saliva that drips from both corners of its mouth, swallows it and then immediately tenses once more.

Celeste struggles not to scream. She knows that the dog won't jump until the man standing beside it tells it to. And although she is sure that the order will not be given, she is appalled by the disgust she feels.

Because the emotion oppressing her now is disgust, rather than fear.

'While I'm here, you needn't be scared of the dog. While I'm here, you needn't be scared of anything,' he says, giving her the most repellent of smiles.

Celeste exhales through her nostrils. She doesn't speak. She looks at the man with the desperate indignation of a hunter's prey.

The shivers running down her spine are more and more frequent now, and harder to control. Her legs want to fold beneath the weight of her own body, which has suddenly become twice as awkward as usual. But for the car she is leaning against, she might already have slipped to her knees on the pavement.

On one other occasion he seized her face with both hands and started kissing her on the mouth, as though in a film. She tried to break away and he stubbornly restrained her. He struck her on the back with a fist and then started kissing her again. Celeste didn't scream, she absorbed all the violence of the impact like a crash-test dummy. The movement he made with his head was horrible.

No, that time, too, what Celeste felt was not fear but rage, a universal and potent rage. And now once again, as she thinks about what happened then, she is intoxicated by a strange feeling of defiance, an irrational masochism that fills her chest, giving her a sense of self-confidence, and indifference to immediate danger. She studies the features of the man in front of her, his pointed nose, his thin body, his complex, hollow eyes, his pale, freckled, almost childish skin, the bright red of his hair, and she's startled by how vile he is.

Grotesque as it might seem, she can clearly detect a sense of disappointment behind her anxiety. Reality, she manages to think, always finds a way of humiliating her most sincerely held convictions, like the belief that a pleasant face cannot conceal malign intentions. She goes on studying him, unable to believe the determination with which he is attempting to terrify her. This man is putting himself forward as protection against an evil for which he is himself responsible.

'Want me to show you how harmless he is?' the man says, stroking the dog's head. Then all of a sudden he purses his lips and strikes the creature with the palm of his hand, on the upper part of its muzzle, between the eyes and nose.

The slap gives a sharp, penetrating sound. Celeste's muscles contract as she awaits a furious reaction on the part of the animal, but it remains passive.

The man holds his smile and lets go of her, cranking up the tension of the moment. Then, without taking his eyes off Celeste, he strikes the dog again, in the same way and at the same point as before, but harder this time.

Finally the Great Dane opens its mouth, revealing an impressive set of teeth coated with thick slobber.

Celeste sees that the dog's eyes are full of tears. For a moment she imagines it as a puppy, trusting and affectionate.

The man slips a hand into the dog's mouth, which remains wide open. Only a few nervous twitches of the tail betray the animal's frustration. A real circus act.

'You saw,' the man says, pulling his hand out. 'I give orders, he obeys. Otherwise I'd take him out to sea and drown him. He knows that.'

Celeste is nauseated, and much more concerned than she imagined. She knows that from this moment on, her days will not be the same. That from today she will have to live on scraps. That henceforth her every initiative, her every movement will be in some way defined by this man's invasive presence.

10

The ringing of the phone insinuates itself into his sleep, still hot with images. At first it is a bearable noise in the middle distance, absorbed by the murmur of guests in a summer garden (a wedding, perhaps, or a christening; in a corner, a string trio is about to strike up); they are people both alive and dead, drinking as they murmur to one another, ignoring David Heller's repeated attempts to break into their conversation.

Only at the fourth ring does his mind isolate and recognise the sound, which makes him start. Still half sunk in the dream that won't let him go, he leaps from the armchair, dragging his body into reality ahead of his mind, which retains a shot of the garden and a few faces, and this unnatural effort, his body's striving for a sensation that he doesn't yet feel, is a blind hunger to survive, an uncontrolled need to return, open his eyes, re-emerge; a tug of war with death that Heller realises he has experienced in the past, and which he wins by a smaller margin each time.

The first thing his eyes register is the spine of the fourth volume of the legal encyclopaedia that occupies an entire shelf in his study library. With his heart beating madly inside him, Heller hurls himself at the phone, which goes on ringing. And he feels very old as he notices how much effort he has to make just to reach his desk.

He picks up the receiver. It's heavier than he remembered.

'David?'

'Yes.'

'David, it's me, Elena.'

'Elena.'

'What's up, are you OK?'

Heller looks at his reflection in the glass of the framed degree certificate on the far wall.

'I'm . . . yeah.'

'You didn't even say hello.'

'I woke up all of a sudden, sorry.'

'No, I'm the one who's sorry. I didn't think I'd be disturbing you at this time of day.'

His rapid heartbeats subside. Heller walks round the desk, sits down in the revolving chair and tries to get his thoughts together.

'No, you did just the right thing. I barely slept last night. I must have been exhausted.'

'Listen, how are you?'

'Oh, fine, I'm doing a lot of work on a new case, a farmer who shot a thief he'd surprised in his garden one night.' Before he continues, he pauses. As though to get to the point. 'But how are you? We haven't seen each other for a while.'

'David, I . . . I've been thinking about calling you for some time. I didn't know whether it was the right thing to do or not.'

Heller has nothing to say in response, or even to change the subject; so he says nothing. He becomes aware that he is trying to send a message with his silence, but he doesn't know what that message might be.

At the other end of the line she hears, for the first time, the effect of the demanding words she has just addressed to him. And she in turn says nothing, creating a frame around what she is about to say.

'David?'

'I'm here.'

'That thing I said to you.'

'What thing?'

'That thing in the car. The evening after the exams, when I drove you home.'

Heller stares at the window, gripped by an irritation stronger than his ability to control it.

He is more unsettled than worried by Elena's concern for him. He is entirely aware of what she's talking about, but he's annoyed that she's doing it. He perceives her interest as an intrusion, an improper form of admission into his life. And he has no wish to explain things to her. In fact, out of an instinctive, stubborn feeling of spite which he doesn't even entirely welcome, he intends to call an immediate halt to her expectations of him.

'Elena, what are you doing? Judging me?'

At the other end, Elena plunges into a bewildered silence of wounded affection.

He waits, keeping his anger in check.

When Elena finally decides to speak, her voice is curt and conclusive.

'A moment ago I said I'd been wondering if it was OK to call you.'

'Elena, wait a moment.'

But she doesn't wait. She doesn't want to hear any more. It's her turn now, and he isn't going to stop her. He isn't going to get out of this by apologising. He won't treat her badly ever again. Perhaps in five, ten minutes, a week, she will regret her need to punish him, And then she'll find a way of making up, she'll smile at him in the lift, perhaps, and he'll say: Elena please I wasn't thinking that time, I was nervous, I really didn't understand what you were talking about, of course I wouldn't refuse to answer you, ask me anything you like, you mustn't be afraid of me, and she will feel an immediate sense of relief, a wound suddenly healed, life returning, it's as though she can already feel the caress of that pleasure and the very thought makes her happy, God how little it would take, we carry such needless pain within ourselves, and the push-button panel of the lift would indicate another floor, then she would throw a bit of a sulk for his benefit, and finally she would allow him a few words: You really know how to be a boor when you want to, I didn't know that side of you and it hasn't exactly been a pleasure. That would be it, and then she'd add that coda, 'It hasn't exactly been a pleasure', which strikes her as having an elegant hauteur to it, and the lift would climb another floor, he would look at her, his head lowered, eyebrows raised as he began to understand, look at him there, a child, that's what he is, like everyone else deep down, Come over here, she would say, freeing a hand and drawing him to her, and he would bury his face in her neck and immediately desire her, an embrace so strong it would hurt, their papers between them, her face between his hands, Ah, no, not here, steady now, have you forgotten where we are? And reaching their floor the lift would begin to come to a rest, he would pull away from her as the doors opened, and the people waiting on the landing would look at them with embarrassment and she, more amused than unsettled, would go out first, he trailing along the corridor in her wake, and he would pause as he walked, saying, Then I'll call you this evening, Fine, she would reply as she reached the door of her office, and then she would enter the room, closing the door behind her to stay alone with her happiness, the happiness she had worked so hard and suffered for and which was now coming to stay.

Yes, she would do that in five minutes, ten minutes, a week. She would work things out in her imagination in those precise terms in five minutes, ten minutes, a week.

But not now. Now she's hurt. Nervous. Humiliated. Treated worse than she deserves. She feels as though she has every reason to be angry. Now she has to respond.

'I have the answer to my question, David, do you want to hear it?'

Heller wants to say something, but he holds himself back. He knows when to keep his mouth shut.

'I've done a bad thing. Very bad.'

And he hangs up.

★

She's sitting on the bed. In front of her, hanging from the wall by the chest of drawers, is a little round mirror.

Without getting up, Elena stretches her neck until the mirror frames her face. She's looking lovely today, what a shame. Before calling him she had combed her hair, she remembers only now. She'd done it for him, even though she knew he wouldn't see her.

The pain comes much sooner than she had hoped. A sweet desolation that spreads inside her as the seconds pass, and then begins to flow into the room, settling on all the objects in it, stripping them of meaning and happiness.

She looks at the telephone on the dressing table. Her resentment has vanished. Irrational though it might seem, she isn't angry with David. And the more she forces herself to become indignant again, the more she realises she has no real anger, that she is entirely unable to feel anything other than affection for him.

Above all she understands, with a sharp pain in her stomach, that her wretched desires, the stupid little images that she spends so much time constructing so carefully, are never going to be fulfilled. That she is too weak compared to him. That he has never held her hand, not once. That he has never kissed her. That there is nothing between them.

And this simple truth that she has been trying to hide from herself for so long and now sees so clearly, rather than persuading her to get him out of her head, makes David Heller take root in her life like a kind of destiny.

11

Ten to eight. Celeste leaves by the front door with her backpack over her shoulder and her hands in her jacket pockets. She walks along the footpath that runs alongside her block, struggling against the temptation to glance back. Only when she reaches the end of the street does she turn around, looking up towards the windows of her flat.

And sure enough, there's her mother, just turning away. She has done that since Celeste went to primary school. She couldn't leave the house without her mother plonking herself in the window and watching after her until the end of the street. And every time she leaves the house, Celeste walks with her head held high, pretending that she doesn't sense with every step she takes, her mother's watchful, unstinting love, a remnant from her childhood, a love that secretly wants stay by her side as she walks away.

She sees the public telephone on the other side of the road, and crosses over to it. She picks up the receiver, takes a prepay card from her pocket and slips it carefully into the belly of the phone, waiting for the machine to suck it in (she's been cheated too often not to know how it's done). She keys in the number, crosses her legs and looks round as she waits.

The glow of the lights of a double-parked car. The resigned face of a young man lifting the shutters of a shop, holding the key firmly in the electronic lock. The sound of the coffee cups in a nearby café. A carpet being beaten against the iron railings of a balcony by a stout woman who purses her lips and turns her head away at each stroke.

Celeste says something into the telephone. She says very little, then she falls silent. Wrinkling her nose, she listens to the reply.

Then she takes the receiver away from her ear. She looks at it.

She hangs up.

As she removes the card, a well-dressed woman walks past her with great dignity. She's pushing a pram. She walks proudly, as though to show everyone how happy she is.

Two women, drawn by her proud walk, stare at her, curious. She slows down a little to let them peer into the pram. They lean over it, then look at each other and walk on, pulling strange faces.

Celeste follows the woman. She crosses the square, walking behind her as far as the bus shelter. The woman stops to rearrange the blankets in the pram. Celeste approaches, pretending she needs to read the timetables on the bus-stop pole. She's already worked out what's going on, but she still leans forward to look. The woman meets her eye and smiles. Then she bends once more over the empty pram.

Celeste boards the first bus that comes. She waves at the woman from the window.

Twenty minutes later she is sitting at a café table, blowing on the foam of a cappuccino. People are constantly coming and going, obstructing Celeste's view of the entrance. She has to keep leaning over to avoid losing sight of the door on the other side of the street.

She knows she won't be able to wait for ever. That the cappuccino won't last for long. That even if she ordered something else, she would have to leave sooner or later. She knows that Heller might already have gone out (although given the time of day it seems reasonable to think that he hasn't left in the twenty minutes it took her to reach his building); that he might come out late, or not come out at all.

She knows, finally, that it will be a matter of chance whether she sees him or not. And that even if he does come out of that door as she hopes he will, she wouldn't know what to do beyond looking at him for a moment or two and then leaving, dazed by her own ineffectuality.

And yet there she stays, letting her cappuccino get cold, waiting for her unformed strategy to come into focus. As though she needed to see Heller right in front of her before she knew what to do next.

But that's the deal. At the very least, she will have begun to learn his schedule. And she's very fond of Heller's building, with its old-fashioned style. The inner courtyard with the stone fountain. That lovely old lift that you can see even from here.

She finishes the cappuccino and stands up. From the adjacent table she picks up the café's newspaper, returns to her table and flicks through it.

The barman comes out from behind the counter and removes her empty cup. Celeste continues scanning the headlines, but in her head she's counting backwards. The barman's tactic, which she has already interpreted as a clear request, has made her impatient.

Bearing in mind that she hasn't been bothering anybody.

And that she was going to have a pastry.

And that the place is almost empty.

She goes and pays the cashier, taking her eyes off the doorway.

She emerges from the bar, nervously counting her change, feeling the pain of all the times she has felt excluded, just like this time, forced to lower her head (or turn away, which amounts to the same thing). For absolutely no reason, no reason at all.

She goes on gripping and rubbing the coins between her fingers as though she wants to break them, while right in front of her Heller is handing an envelope to the porter, repeating the name of the person he wants him to deliver it to.

When Celeste looks up, mechanically focusing straight ahead, she sees a man she thinks she ought to recognise. Then she turns this way and that, trying hard to remember why she has come here.

Heller crosses the street, passing so close to her that she can smell his aftershave. Celeste collects herself and turns her face away as though fearful of being discovered.

Heller stops by the entrance to a garage a little further along. He calls someone by name in a loud voice. Aldo or Angelo, Celeste can't quite make it out.

A moment later a boy in his twenties, fair and chubby, with the sleeves of his jumper rolled up to his elbows and his jeans slipped into a pair of long rubber boots, comes out onto the footpath clutching a bunch of keys.

A few metres away Celeste keys a number into her mobile, raises it to her ear, nods in response to the recorded voice telling her how much credit she has left, and explodes into a series of phrases: 'Where are you, I can hardly hear you'; 'Did you say Saturday afternoon?'; 'No, I can't make it tomorrow'; while all the while looking intently at Heller.

Their eyes meet for a moment, but it's an encounter born out of proximity, entirely meaningless, between two strangers paying no heed to one another.

Heller is wearing a charcoal suit slightly too large for him, which seems to follow him as he moves, but after a slight delay, enfolding him in a kind of agreeable casualness. Rectangular sunglasses, with small, flat lenses. His hair combed back, long enough to cover the back of his neck. A slightly battered leather briefcase.

'It's ready, Avvocato Heller, it's parked outside,' says the mechanic, handing him his car keys. And he walks ahead along the pavement to show Heller exactly where it is.

Celeste takes a few steps in their direction with her phone still pressed to her ear, miming the reaction she might make if her connection started breaking up, and moving around abruptly as if trying to get it back.

The boy goes back inside almost immediately. Heller waves the keys in the air searching for the remote control for his car alarm. A moment later the locks click open. Celeste comes a little closer. Heller opens the back door, takes off his jacket (his tie flips up and drapes over his right shoulder), and throws it inside the car along with his briefcase, opens the front door and climbs in. Celeste quickens her pace and then slows down again. Heller switches on the engine, adjusts the rear-view mirror, and turns the wheel. The indicator blinks and the car joins the traffic. Remaining on the pavement, Celeste walks beside the car and imprints it in her memory. Without looking round, she follows it into the square where the street ends. Then she stops to watch it disappear down a long tree-lined avenue.

An angry whistle, apparently directed at her.

She's in the middle of the street.

A red light straight in front of her.

Ten metres away, the cars begin to pull away.

Some hysterical hooting.

Celeste reaches the other side of the street, running, almost ending up in the arms of the traffic policewoman who glares at her in disapproval, thrusting into the girl's face the hand with which she has just stopped the traffic especially for her.

'Sorry,' says Celeste, 'I was distracted.'

'Go on, then,' the woman says forgivingly. And she waves her forearm like a windscreen wiper towards the cars, which would continue on their way even without her needless intervention.

Celeste adjusts her backpack, walks randomly for a few metres, stops, folds her arms and rests her chin in the palm of her right hand. She thinks again about Heller's clothes. About his haste. About the job he does.

Where else could he be going? she says to herself. More as an affirmation than an inquiry.

She checks her watch.

A short distance away she sees the M of the metro.

Let's give it a try, she thinks.

She has never been in a law court before. She is disoriented by all these corridors, although she doesn't dislike the place. It feels almost like a shopping centre, with its café, its display cabinets (although they contain only books), the escalator, the lifts, the offices, the porters loading and unloading. People greeting one another, chatting, laughing over an amusing piece of information or expressing regret over a sad one, walking together for a few moments and then parting.

You can tell the lawyers at a glance by the similarity of their clothes, their attitudes and the way they walk, the movements of their bodies when they meet, form little groups and chat. All coming and going. All acting as if they're about to run out of time. Perhaps they aren't actually in all that much of a hurry. Some of them walk thoughtfully along the corridors with their hands clasped behind their backs, acting out a self-confidence rendered even more artificial by the gowns they wear.

Celeste smiles at the thought that she might at any moment spot a familiar face. Her punters don't tend to greet her in situations such as this, and oddly enough they are always keen to apologise to her the next time they come back.

When that happens she teasingly denies that any such encounter had ever taken place (Oh, really? What, the other day? Where?) and sees them retreat, disappointed and filled with an obscure sense of inferiority that they can do nothing about.

They always ask to make love immediately. To get in there as quickly as possible.

She satisfies their desires. Sometimes she hasn't even time to take her knickers off. She just pushes them aside with her fingers to let them inside her, so aroused are they by their anger. But she isn't bothered by their greediness. She insists only that they don't bite her, stupidly starving as they are. That they don't leave marks. Only on that condition can they come back. And they actually respect her wishes.

Celeste looks around. Still walking, she finds herself back at the entrance. She is surprised to have circled the whole floor without noticing. The security guard is there, standing by the screen that shows the contents of the bags passing through the X-ray machine. Celeste met him a short time ago.

'Where do you think you're going?' he said to her then, after waiting for her to pick her backpack up from the rollers.

Celeste gave him a look for a moment and he, still

staring at his monitor, pointed to a sheet of paper on the wall that said 'This entrance is reserved for lawyers, magistrates and court staff'; and while she stood as though transfixed he concluded with the pomposity of an inspector: 'What's up, can't you read?'

Without deigning to glance at her.

Celeste lifted her middle finger. All of a sudden the man turned. She whisked the finger away, flashing the most idiotic smile she could muster.

He let her in.

From the end of the corridor comes an agitated sound of moving bodies.

'Let them through, come on, now, let them through,' someone says, and then there is the sing-song sound of a woman's voice, calling repeatedly: 'Just a moment, stop for just a moment, please.'

Celeste turns, as do the other people around her. All activity in this part of the building is suspended, like a single frame flickering on the screen when the film gets caught in a projector. From a distance, Celeste sees only blurred bodies which seem to draw towards one another before pulling suddenly apart. Then she recognises the uniforms of two policemen, and a handcuffed man between them. They walk on, ponderous and obedient, holding the prisoner by the arms; and whether they are aware of it or not their downcast faces, their desire not to be watched while performing their task, betray the age-old unease of the henchman.

Celeste leans against the wall as they pass in front of

her. The woman who was calling to them to stop is silent now. Now she simply walks beside them, holding a child of five or six by the hand.

Slowly, almost mechanically, Celeste follows them. The policemen take the stairs, even though there is a lift available right beside them. Following regulations, Celeste thinks to herself.

The woman stops as they climb the stairs. The little boy grips her arm with both hands, rocking exhaustedly back and forth. The prisoner turns towards her, just once. The woman looks at him bravely.

'Come on,' says the policeman walking ahead of him, with a note of sympathy in his voice. Then they disappear behind the first flight of stairs.

The woman turns in the direction of the lift, which is still free, tugs the little boy by the arm and moves towards it. Celeste does the same. She says thank you when she enters the lift. The woman keeps her finger on the button and looks into Celeste's eyes for a moment, as though to ask if she's pressing for the right floor. Celeste nods. As the lift ascends, she smiles at the little boy, who is staring at her. She is attracted by his dignity. By the clean smell emanating from the few clothes he is wearing. By the half-moon scar at the base of his neck, which she thinks looks like an old man's mouth.

The little boy, still hanging like a deadweight from his mother's arm, makes faces at himself in the mirror. Three times he leans over to touch it with his lips, three times she covers his mouth with her hand at the last minute.

When the lift reaches their floor, a little waiting crowd

of people fall upon it, so impatient to get through the opening doors that, stupidly, they block the exit.

Shouting 'Excuse me,' the woman opens a path through the people, clearing her way with her son. Startled by this display of bad manners, Celeste watches the woman disappear down the corridor past the courtrooms, as she herself struggles to leave. By the time she is out of the lift, Celeste has already given up hope of finding her again. She looks around, noticing to her surprise that this floor is much quieter than the one she has just left. In the distance she sees two policemen guarding a courtroom. They don't look like the ones that accompanied the woman's husband.

She walks slowly, trying to grow accustomed to her new environment. She feels slightly uneasy, as though she has no right to be here, and at any moment someone might ask her who let her in. There is a strong smell of wood and old papers, and far fewer people than were circulating down below.

A man in his shirtsleeves is handing sheets of paper to a woman, giving her serious instructions, or at least that is what is suggested by the haste with which she goes off in the opposite direction, clutching the pile that the man has handed to her. The soles of her moccasins slip swiftly down the corridor floor. From a short distance away, her unstable, jerky motion almost makes her look like a bad skater.

Standing by a stall of legal texts, a sales rep in a jacket and tie looks around and waits.

Drawn by the amplified voices coming clearly from

the hall at the end of the corridor, Celeste stops to listen more closely. One voice relates the sequence of events leading up to a scene of bloody pandemonium; another, more authoritative, interrupts the first from time to time, correcting individual words or pointing out an overstatement in the reconstruction. Then the first voice stops, apologises and continues, dwelling on the subject of a man's persistence in gripping the barrel of a rifle aimed straight at him through the bars of a window.

Intrigued, Celeste hurries towards the courtroom. The policemen she saw from a distance are talking to one another a few feet from a dark doorway, lit only by a chink of light running down the middle. Further off, a gowned lawyer is explaining something in a whisper to three people who are listening attentively to him. Celeste stops at the entrance and gently pushes the right-hand door.

The first thing she sees is a man snoozing behind a large raised bench, one hand resting on top of the other, a tricolour sash worn diagonally over his jacket. She leans a little further forward, and sees two more men decorated in the same manner. She has just enough time to notice the gowns of the two magistrates sitting in the middle of the semicircular bench, when the voice of one of the policemen takes her by surprise.

'Can I help you?'

Here we go, thinks Celeste.

'Can I help you?' the policeman repeats, coming closer as Celeste turns round.

'I wanted to go in,' she says, raising her thumb towards the door, 'if I may,' she adds.

'Are you related to somebody?' the policeman asks, standing directly in front of her.

'Meaning what?' Celeste asks (Is there such a thing as a policeman without a moustache? she thinks).

'Do you have a personal interest in the trial?' the policeman inquires. It sounds like one of those formal phrases that are designed for use in particular circumstances. The strange thing is, whenever you hear them uttered in real life, it's as if their meaning ought to be perfectly clear, although of course it isn't.

'No,' says Celeste, far from sure that she has understood the question. In fact, come to think of it, it's even more ambiguous than the last one.

'Might I ask why you want to go in?'

'It's for college,' Celeste improvises. 'A dissertation. And surely trials are public, are they not?'

The policeman rubs his gums with his tongue for a moment.

'The public entrance is on the other side,' he says finally, using his index finger to draw an imaginary bridge next to Celeste's head.

'Where, over there?' she asks, turning round. But she sees no other doors. Puzzled, she looks at the policeman again.

'Turn right, first door you come to. Not the one ahead of you, but on one side. Court of Assizes. It's written on the door.'

At that precise moment Celeste recognises Heller's

voice at the microphone. How could she not have noticed before?

'Why can't you let me in by this one?' she asks.

'Because this is the magistrates' entrance.'

'Oh. First on the right, you said,' Celeste says as she turns to go.

The policeman nods, without much conviction. He has one more question to ask her: 'You are eighteen, aren't you?'

'Didn't I say I'm at college?'

'Mm,' says the policeman.

And finally he lets her go.

There's a weary atmosphere in the room. And a stale, sickly smell that is at first almost impossible to bear. The hearing has clearly been under way for some time. As she tries to find a seat among the spectators, Celeste wonders why they don't open the windows, at least a little.

From his raised bench the chairman of the court, his hands beneath his desk and his upper body leaning forward slightly, seems to have his eye on everything that happens in the courtroom. He has a pleasant, elderly face. The other gowned judge, sitting beside him but slightly lower down, holds his face in his hands and follows the trial with suspicious eyes. Of the six jury members seated around them, in two groups, some stifle yawns, some wear reasonably detached expressions, while others grip at the edge of their desks to sharpen their concentration.

Celeste chooses a place from which she has a side view of Heller. A weird position he's chosen to speak from. It strikes her as odd that neither the chairman nor the judge who's assisting him has anything to say about it. An implicit acknowledgement of his professional competence, she imagines.

Meanwhile he has taken off his gown and folded it up on the bench, partially covering his case file, as though he doesn't need to refer to it during his address. He is standing up, but with one knee resting on his chair, placing his body at an oblique angle that seems to relate to his intention to launch a surprise attack on the people he is speaking to. His voice is rather low but very clear, and he has a sinuous way of gesticulating, as though stroking his words.

Sitting at the next bench, the public prosecutor looks the other way, granting him a vaguely resentful look from time to time.

'Ladies and gentlemen of the jury, you are in an unenviable position. You come from a society that works to live, goes on holiday once a year, comes home tired every evening and starts the whole process all over again from the beginning every day,' says Heller, looking around the room, lingering for a moment on each face.

Even those who are dozing raise their heads.

'This is probably the first trial that you have attended. Your knowledge of the law is limited to your respect for it; or perhaps to the trust you place in it. But they have made you put on this tricolour sash – and this, whether you like it or not, makes you judges. Today, whether you wish to or not, you will make a decision about a person's life. And however much you may try to convince yourselves, quite understandably, that you have only a small part to play in this trial, you must be aware that this is not the case. The decision that you come to in this courtroom will be of very great significance. It will have consequences that will impact on this man's life, his family, his career. And precisely because you will have to make your decision lacking the technical competence of the two magistrates sitting at the centre of this bench, your task will be twice as difficult as theirs.'

Here Heller sighs sagely.

'It is not an easy situation to be in, I am aware of that. Not easy at all.'

And he stops, giving his last sentence time to settle in the receptive minds of the jury members. When he resumes, it is as though he is beginning his second chapter.

'I am defending the accused man. I have the strength of my conviction, and many years of professional experience to back me up. For this reason, every word I say may influence you, work on your sense of responsibility and make your decision more difficult in one direction or another. I am aware, then, that you need me no less than I need you. So let us hold our hands out to one another. Let us help each other to understand what really happened in this terrible story. I promise to lay it all out clearly, and you may take it or leave it as seems right to you.'

Celeste folds her arms. She is aware of the universal

feeling of respect that Heller is producing in his audience.

'You already know quite enough about the defendant,' Heller says, turning towards the sunburnt old man sitting on a bench behind him. 'You have seen and heard him during the preliminary statement to the court. He is a farmer who owns a smallholding. You know, the type that stands by the motorway, with little two-storey buildings that are never quite finished, and aluminium fittings that you can see standing out against the concrete. So, the defendant is one of those many people we see for a moment out of our car windows, usually bending over to pull something out of the ground.'

A few heads begin to nod. A lady member of the jury cranes her neck as far as possible in Heller's direction, as though she wished to enlarge his image.

'And this farmer, old, in poor health and the owner of a smallholding, stands before you now for the killing a thief.'

The chairman smiles, accepting Heller's decision to admit from the outset the perpetration of what is unarguably an offence, in order to gain credibility in the eyes of the court. His face hardens only right at the end of the sentence, when he is clearly irritated by Heller's attempt to play down the gravity of the crime by describing its victim in pejorative terms. He looks out of the corner of his eye for the associate judge, to share his disappointment with him, but by now the lawyer has already reached his goal.

'He surprised him at night, in his garden,' Heller

resumes, 'and fired at him with a hunting rifle through the bars of a window.'

And here Heller falls silent, allowing his gaze to wander along the faces of the jury.

'Why did he do it? That is the question I can still read in your faces. He could have called the police. Used the rifle only to threaten. Or even better, threatened the man with an unloaded rifle. That would have proved that he had no intention to harm. Anyone who picks up a loaded rifle, you must surely be thinking, is by that very act demonstrating a violent intention. And that is entirely true.'

'We can see where you're taking this,' is the phrase that seemed imprinted on the faces of judges and jury. Or judges at least.

'I don't know where you live, Mr Chairman, magistrates, ladies and gentlemen of the jury. It may be that some of you live in the country. Many people have chosen to leave the city so as to breathe a little better and look at a tree from time to time.'

As Heller speaks he gives the appearance of constructing his argument as he goes along, creating an effect of spontaneity that makes him appear to be more interested in the truth than in absolving his client. Celeste realises that she too is sensitive to this impression.

'Well,' Heller begins again, 'some years ago, you will of course remember, in the hills that surround our city there was a new outbreak of burglaries at private homes. One sensational case involved a well-known dentist who tried to defend his family against burglars who entered his home in broad daylight. They killed him in the kitchen, with a metal orange press.'

'You know, I do remember that,' say the faces of almost all those present in the courtroom. Some of them even whisper the name of the murdered man.

'I have a close friend who works as an estate agent,' the lawyer continues, smoothly assuming a more relaxed tone. 'It was during that period that his company recorded the greatest rise in the number of rural properties for sale that it had ever experienced. Many sellers actually wanted to exchange their villas for small flats, in condominiums and in areas of high-density housing. These people had lost any sense of security living in their own homes, and were willing to reassess their ideas of domestic comfort just to regain that sense of security.'

The chairman folds his arms.

'It has never happened to me, gentlemen of the court, but I think it must be terrible to find yourself at home and to feel your blood suddenly freeze at the thought that you might have left a window open. You end up living in a state of constant anxiety. Anxiety made all the more unbearable by the fact that it settles in the very place where we should find comfort, making half-closed doors look threatening, making the very walls seem hostile.'

Many people begin to nod. Celeste feels a churning mixture of excitement and repulsion. Absurd as it may seem, she has a sense that Heller believes in what he is saying.

'In the face of this kind of anxiety, the possible solutions are very simple. Those who can do so sell up and buy elsewhere. And enrich estate agents in the process. Those who can't, stay where they are. And defend themselves. Arm themselves if necessary. If they find themselves facing a danger from which there is no escape.'

The public prosecutor, one eyebrow raised, taps his desk with his fingernails. Heller gives him a sidelong glance and a hint of a smile, before turning back to face the court.

'I know that the public prosecutor has done everything within his power to make you resist the temptation of a defence of "legitimate force". His argument is a simple one: there was an iron grille between the defendant and his attacker, so the concrete and actual danger required by the law to support legitimate force was, in this case, absent.'

The associate judge sinks smugly into the back of his armchair.

'But what is danger, I ask you? Is it a certainty, or is it rather the reasonable possibility that serious harm might be done? How many times have we underestimated the extent of a danger, realising when it was already too late that we should have raised the threshold of our caution? Danger, ladies and gentlemen, is a matter of conjecture. Of hypothesis.'

Even the chairman is nodding now. The associate judge cranes his neck towards Heller with the alertness of a hunting dog.

'Let us reconstruct the facts. The defendant surprises a stranger in his garden, in the dead of night. He is afraid. He has heard of too many dreadful incidents that have occurred in houses like his own. He picks up his rifle, and aims it at the intruder through the grille fixed over a ground-floor window. He tells him to leave. The man could leave, but instead he confronts the defendant and threatens him. He provokes him. I would ask you to read his words carefully, in the police statement: "Shoot, you old fool. Don't you see that you're not up to it? You don't scare me with your rifle, if I want to get in, I'll get in. And if you want I'll show you right now." And he grips the rifle by the barrel. "Go on, show me what you can do, old man." He mocks his weapon. He incites him. He persists with his threat: "If I want to get in, I'll get in."'

Celeste gets to her feet. All of a sudden, she doesn't know why, she has had enough. She makes for the door, but she doesn't leave quite yet.

'Do you really believe that this kind of criminal taunting would not produce, in someone under threat, and an old person at that, the conviction of imminent danger? It matters little whether the intruder really could have entered the defendant's house. What matters in that moment is that the defendant was right to think that he could have. Thus the sense of danger. Thus the legitimate force. Thus the fatal shot fired during this awful struggle taking place between the bars of the window.'

The public prosecutor looks with interest at Heller,

then tries to get the lawyer's thesis into some sort of perspective by moving his head from side to side. But the chairman freezes him with a glance. He is one of those judges who refuse to allow any form of overt calculation in the courtroom.

'It cannot be denied that what we see here is a disproportionate reaction,' Heller admits. 'Disproportionate given the circumstances of the crime. Criminal negligence is involved.'

The chairman and the associate judge exchange glances.

'Let us examine these concepts in greater detail.'

The members of the jury faithfully wait for Heller's explanation.

'Criminal negligence, ladies and gentlemen of the jury, is a distinct form of moral culpability. Under penal law, the negligent person is free of intent. He does not wish to commit his crime. Malice corresponds to culpability in law. Negligence is, we might say, a benign tumour. It is the unwilled act that contradicts the intention. So this is what the accused has done: convinced that he was acting in legitimate self-defence, he erred on the side of negligence. I trust that none of you believes that the defendant *wished* to kill. If we are here today, it is solely to establish the extent to which he must answer for the death that he has caused. And it is my sincere conviction that we have before us a case of accidental excessive force in putative legitimate defence, based, that is, on the reasonable conviction of a present danger. For this reason, I ask you to reach a formal verdict of not guilty. My analysis of the legal situation is contained in the statement of defence which I have presented for the attention of the court. Thank you.'

Celeste leaves the courtroom as the judges and the jury rise and start to make their way to the council chamber. She has had enough of the ceremonial atmosphere, the whiff of the sacristy.

She walks back down the corridor, which is slightly less busy than it was when she arrived. She enters the empty lift and presses the button marked T - for Terra - heading for the ground floor.

The doors open onto a view that she does not recognise. Celeste steps out of the lift and walks into the corridor in front of her.

There is very little light, a series of half-open doors, piles of large boxes stacked at the bottom of the walls, rusty trolleys and worn-out old chairs. A little natural light filters into one room at the end of the corridor.

Celeste starts back towards the lift, but it has already been called. She sees the number four flashing. At that moment she realises she is frightened.

She looks around in the hope of finding some stairs. There are none. She turns back towards the corridor. Not a sound. Come on, she says to herself. The stairs must be on that side. And if they aren't, come back to the lift and wait.

She has walked almost the entire length of the corridor when she hears the sound of a door opening some distance behind her. She turns around. The silhouette of a man, bending slightly forward, who first moves his head as though to see her better, and then comes towards her.

Celeste glances around in both directions. To her right, a wall. To her left another corridor, darker than this one. And the stairs?

She puts her hand in her pocket and takes out the little box of mints that she always carries with her. She slides back the little flap to open it. Taking care not to cut herself, she slips out the razor blade hidden below the sweets. She holds it firmly between her thumb and her index finger, puts her hand back in her pocket and waits for the man.

She feels better. The blade gives her a sense of security, which is why she never parts with it.

The man comes closer. Celeste presses her back against the wall. She takes her hand from her pocket and holds it in readiness by her thigh.

The man emerges into the faint glow of the few functioning bulbs that hang from the ceiling on dusty wires. He is much shorter than he seemed from a distance; physically squat, not much hair, a blue jacket. He stops a few feet away from Celeste and leans his head to one side to get a better look.

'Excuse me, Miss, did you press the button marked T?'

'What?' says Celeste.

'This is the basement. At least ten times a day I have to come and collect people who've pressed the wrong button. And why wouldn't they, when it's written wrongly in the lift?'

'Oh,' says Celeste, putting her hand back in her pocket. 'And how do I get out now?'

'If you don't want to wait for the lift, the stairs are at the end on the right, just past the other corridor. But be careful, because you can hardly see a thing.'

'Thanks,' says Celeste, and follows his directions.

12

Heller drives home shortly after three. The streets, almost deserted at this time of the afternoon, seem to conspire with him to make his journey even more pleasant than usual. He looks at his hands, which stroke the steering wheel, still warm from the sun it absorbed in the car park, and he is so pleased with himself that he feels he is bringing an aesthetic quality even to the act of driving, as though he were doing it in a very special way.

He hasn't forgotten his fear. Not for a moment. He has it in his briefcase, in one of the inside pockets into which he slipped the scissored scrap of rucksack. But it isn't causing him quite so much pain now. For the first time in days he realises that he is managing to apply the rigid logic of the criminal lawyer to himself, reducing the accusation to its essentials and stabbing it right in the heart, shedding as little blood as possible.

He says to himself: Talk to yourself as you would talk to a client you were defending. This person saw you, so? He has the child (or what's left of her at this point), so? You've left no clues, you're sure of that. You've been as alert as possible, as always. Granted, there is always a margin of error to be taken into account (and bear in mind that at the moment this is the only one of your worries that has any real foundation), but that would be true in any case, even if no one had seen you, followed you and left that message in your mailbox. What else is worrying you – the rucksack? You weren't stupid enough to touch it with your bare hands. Even on the beach you were careful to let it slip from your shoulders, and you shoved it under the boat with your foot. Paradoxical though it might seem, your enemy has nothing to work with. Certainly, he could report you (and if he did so it would be his word against yours), but that's not what he wants. He would have done that already. And the more time that passes without anyone discovering the little girl (you check the papers every day, and they still haven't mentioned it), the more unlikely it becomes that this is his intention. Evidence from any traces you might have left on her would undoubtedly have been more reliable if analysed immediately, rather than several days later. So, be calm and wait. Time is on your side. Let him come when he will. Listen to his requests and judge your responses carefully. Don't fall into his trap. Because that's exactly what you've been doing so far. You've let fear take hold of you. You've let your mind be clouded.

Heller has done well, acting out his role as a lawyer like any other. And as he contemplates the impeccable sequence of propositions that he has presented, he realises that the coherence of his analysis leaves him entirely indifferent, like a patient listening with resignation as the doctor tells him he's fine, while he remains constantly aware of the symptoms of the hidden illness he alone understands.

But if for a moment he abandons the cold logic with which he seeks to defend himself, he discovers within himself a graver apprehension than the fear of punishment and prison. Like the premonition of a disaster that he cannot escape and, to make matters even worse, a disaster which part of him – the part that for some days now has been taking the upper hand – fully expects at any moment. And although he tries to pretend that he is taking part in the life of the city that pulses within him at this time of the afternoon, as though he were simply one of the many who live here, he knows very well that as soon as he closes his front door that sense of expectation will return and assault him, recalling images of little bodies trussed like lambs, cleaned, washed and dead, and the tearing off of the adhesive tape that compresses and conceals, and that expression of disappointment that he can't erase even by spreading it with his hands, and the nights with the light left on, the smell of his dreams, the days starting over, the noise, the people, the case files, the court, the defendants, the sentences and indictments.

It'll have to come to an end, all this. He's so tired.

Perhaps it's coming to an end already. That's what he feels.

But right now he's enjoying cruising the half-empty streets as though the future didn't concern him so much. He listens to the hum of the engine, checks the alternating movements of his feet on the pedals, changes

gear at each bend and is contented. In his childhood –
the period in his life when he looked on the world of
adults as the world of difficulty and responsibility - he
thought he would never learn to drive.

And look how good he is at it now. Just look at that
skill!

Sitting in the kitchen, Celeste is eating the last of the
fruit. Her mother, standing between the table and the
sink, is tidying up. She has poor coordination, and
moves with incomplete, incoherent gestures. A body
expressing an intention that she can't quite bring herself
to carry out. She opens the crockery cupboard, slides in
two glasses, one inside the other, turns around, waves her
hands in the air as though she suddenly needs something, reopens the crockery cupboard and separates the
two glasses.

Celeste avoids her eye. She knows a question is on the
way. She also knows what it's going to be, almost
certainly. She piles the fruit peel in the middle of her
plate, picks it up with both hands and gets up from the
table.

Finally her mother makes up her mind.

'Can you tell me why you don't do your homework
at home like everyone else?'

Here it comes, Celeste thinks, and tries not to roll her
eyes to the ceiling, a gesture that she can't bear when
other people do it to her.

'I can concentrate harder in the library. It's quiet there,
the phone doesn't ring, and I make better use of my

time,' she replies, opening the door of the cupboard under the sink and emptying her plate into the bin.

'Leave that, I'll do it,' her mother says, taking it out of her hand.

Why? Celeste thinks. But she doesn't try to stop her.

Her mother puts the plate in the sink and turns on the tap.

'And your father and I hardly ever see you.'

'Oh come on, Mum, please,' says Celeste, leaving the kitchen.

She goes into the sitting room. Her father is sitting by the window gazing at the building opposite. Celeste leans against a wall and stares at his back. He seems so calm, so settled in the midst of everything. There he sits, silhouetted against the light. A life that consists solely of seeing and breathing. For two years he has spent his afternoons like that. He never needs anything. Perhaps he's actually happy.

All of a sudden, she doesn't know why, Celeste finds herself choking on a lump in her throat. It's so powerful that she has to swivel her jaw to send it back down to wherever it came from. Her father does something with his head, as though he has noticed he is being watched. But he doesn't even turn around.

Until she hears her mother clattering around randomly, Celeste stands there and watches her father watching. When the noises in the kitchen subside, she goes to her room and gets ready to go out.

★

His elbows on the table, David Heller covers his face with his hands and rocks his head back and forth. Each time his eyes re-emerge from behind the shutters of his fingers, the effort to open them seems greater, as though their passage had somehow aged them.

Heller strokes today's case file. The public prosecutor will appeal, that much is certain. The look on his face.

He thinks once again of his client's gleaming eyes. The moment he took Heller's hands, trying to bring them to his lips. And when Heller, as delicately as possible, extricated himself from that ancient, submissive impulse, offering the man his hand to channel his gratitude into something more dignified, the man clutched it with a strength that was impressive in such an old body, so much so that Heller had to give him two claps on the back to make him relax his hold a little. When he caught the smell of the man's rough skin, like some underground root, he smiled affectionately at the indistinct words his client was slobbering between sobs in his ear, in a dialect, mushy with emotion, that sounded even richer than one might have expected.

Heller gets up, puts the file back in the cabinet, takes a step back and looks at the spines of his current case files. With a swift glance he ranks them in order of importance. And this is the moment he feared. He certainly isn't short of work, but none of his current jobs calls for the level of application of the one he has just brought to its conclusion.

Wearily he leaves his study. He goes into the bedroom and opens the wardrobe. There on the bottom shelf is the bag of clothes that he put to one side a few days before, waiting to make up his mind whether or not to get rid of them. He looks at the bag without a great deal of conviction. Then he thinks: Yes, OK.

He steps towards the door, sets the bag down on the floor in the hall, and takes his jacket from the coat-rack. He has one arm in a sleeve when the phone rings. Heller glances at his watch. Four-thirty. He frowns, filled suddenly with a familiar flash of indignation. Oh, no, he says to himself. Not again. Then he heads towards the source of the ringing, excited by the prospect of flying off the handle if it really is the phone call he is expecting.

'Avvocato Heller?'

Heller shuts his eyes slowly and opens them with a start. He feels his forehead growing damp.

'Look, don't tell me it's you again. Don't even try,' he replies, aware that he has already raised his voice. He takes off his jacket and lays it on the desk.

'Come on, Avvocato, don't be like that,' the girl replies with patient impertinence. 'I'm only asking for a minute of your time.'

Heller takes the cordless phone away from his ear and looks at it as though it were a foreign body. He can scarcely believe that this intrusive little girl, this artless cold-caller, is mocking his fury. Even with his sense obscured by indignant frustration, he can't help wondering how he could have been so stupid, failing to understand that he was behaving in the worst possible way for someone trying to clinch a deal. He wants to scream, but a spark of common sense persuades him to retreat into a manly, inquisitorial tone.

'What's your name? You tell me your name, first.'

A question, followed by an order. The girl immediately becomes more compliant.

'I really don't understand why you're being so aggressive towards me, Mr Heller. You were last time, too . . .'

'I asked you your name. How are we going to do this, will you tell me or shall I find out for myself?' Heller continues. And he looks at the caller's number on the display panel of his phone.

'I'm just trying to do my job. All I want to do is offer you a case of our finest wine.'

Heller sits down at the desk, by the computer. The girl falls silent when she hears the beep as it switches on.

'What are you doing, Mr Heller?'

'Don't worry, you'll read about it when it comes to court,' says the lawyer. And he connects to the telephone directory website.

'Surely you're not going to report me for offering you a case of wine?'

Heller works the silence, filling it with the click of the mouse from time to time. He goes to the page that allows him to check the caller's name. He keys in the number, which he has written down on a piece of paper.

'I really think it would be a good idea to listen to me, Mr Heller.'

The girl's tone has become very different.

'What?' says Heller, surprised.

At that moment the caller's name appears on the screen.

'You've understood me very well.'

Heller blanches as he reads the words on the computer screen. Café Corsale, 24 Via dell'Addolorata. He jumps to his feet, runs to the window and looks down. His heart flutters in his chest like a crazed bird.

'What are you saying, who are you, what are you talking about?'

No reply.

'Hello!' says Heller, putting his jacket back on and moving towards the hall.

'Going out already?' the girl says. She speaks her words slowly, one at a time.

Heller doesn't reply. His hand freezes on the door handle, and he looks around hopelessly.

'At a table inside, near the window,' she goes on.

'I don't see why I should meet you,' Heller says quickly, thinking on his feet.

'Come down,' Celeste says.

13

David Heller has been a regular at his local café for more than twenty years. Leaving the house, crossing the street, drinking his first coffee, exchanging a couple of words with the cashier and leafing through the morning paper are entirely habitual. Rather like moving from the sitting room to the kitchen. So the strange feeling that strikes him as he looks at the pavement before him involves a keen sense of loss.

He can still clearly hear the voice of his intellect repeatedly telling him not to go, not to appear so tractable from the outset, to wait a little. He listens, in perfect agreement with the voice, and he doesn't care. He knows he should demonstrate that he is stronger than his blackmailer and wait for his response, so that he can study his moves and prepare his own attack. But all he wants right now is to know who he is up against and what awaits him. And in this rashness, this recklessness, he discovers a vast and unexpected feeling of liberation, freeing the hurt that he has kept hidden for so long, and which he finally feels he is sharing with someone.

He takes a deep breath and crosses the road.

After his first few steps, he is filled with a sense of foreboding. As though in crossing that brief stretch of road he is fulfilling a rite of passage. As though, from that moment on, everything is destined to change. Instinctively Heller turns around, as if to say goodbye to his building, with all that such a gesture involves. And for the second time that day he finds the same phrase in his head.

All this is coming to an end.

When he walks into the café he doesn't see anyone sitting at the first few tables. Then he remembers the precise directions: 'A table inside, near the window.'

The cashier is busy sorting out the small change in the drawer of the till. She looks up and smiles at him.

'We missed you this morning,' she says hospitably.

From the counter Heller picks up a newspaper that has been crumpled by many hands. He quickly scans the headlines on the front page.

'Yes. An early session,' he replies.

He folds the paper and puts it back down. Then he walks towards the inside tables, trying to ignore his racing heartbeat.

'Have a seat, Avvocato! What can I get you?' the barman asks from behind the counter.

'Nothing, thanks,' Heller replies, still walking. Then he changes his mind. He raises his right hand without turning round.

'In fact I will. A coffee, no sugar.'

As he enters the inner room of the café, the first thing that draws his attention is the telephone on the wall. Celeste is there, sitting at a circular table with her back to the window. She looks at him with the eyes of a cornered rat, and waits.

She is wearing her hair pulled back into a shabby bandana, a blue round-neck sweater with no shirt, worn-out jeans. Platform-soled rubber boots, visibly heavy for her slender legs. On a chair not far away, a little backpack full of paper, half covered by a denim jacket with a fake woollen lining around the collar.

Heller stops in the doorway. His mind drains for a moment, then starts working once more. Is this, he thinks with a hint of disappointment, the source of my anxiety? Is this badly dressed little girl the reason I have suffered sleepless nights and endured interminable afternoons, and worked to the point of exhaustion just to keep my mind employed? Look at her. She can't be eighteen. And she's a plain little thing. How on earth did they get her involved, dressed like that?

He sits down.

Celeste has an empty glass in front of her, stained on the inside by a fresh residue of orange juice. Between her fingers she holds the slice of lemon that decorated the rim.

Heller makes himself comfortable in one of the positions he assumes in the courtroom when listening to the public prosecutor's closing speech: hands clasped between his supple legs, torso leaning slightly to the right, his facial expression deliberately distracted. He almost regrets facing an adversary who isn't a match for him. But what if there was someone else behind the girl? What if she was merely bait?

'Can I have five minutes of your time?' Celeste asks.

Heller folds his arms. Leaning his head to one side, he

adopts an expression of childish petulance, an indifference too affected to be real. Celeste, on the other hand, doesn't take her eyes off him, and he is struck by her utter front. As though he had been too quick to underestimate her.

'I never buy things on the phone,' he replies. 'I've got to see the product first.'

'Fair enough,' she says in a measured tone, to show him that she has understood. Then she stares at him again, just as she did before.

At this point Heller finds himself thinking how different her voice sounds now. Suggestive, alert. Only at the end of her sentences does he perceive a touch of the adolescent (that clean resonance), but it is a candour that in no way detracts from her femininity, which he recognises as surprisingly adult.

Celeste brings the slice of lemon to her mouth, touches it slightly with the tip of her tongue and bites into it. Heller feels a sharp twinge of unease.

'So have you got the goods you want to show me?' he asks her, returning to the subject.

Celeste stiffens, wounded, as though someone had said something terrible to her. She doesn't reply, so Heller keeps going: 'And how much is it? It all comes down to the price, doesn't it?'

At that moment the barman arrives with his coffee. Heller only becomes aware of the man when the cup is already in front of him, with the bill beside it.

'Here you are, Avvocato. No sugar, as you said. Anything else for you, Miss?'

Celeste shakes her head. And as the barman bows slightly and leaves, Heller gives her a sidelong glance and nods, as though to acknowledge that she has just scored a point.

'Well done,' he says at last.

He is entirely aware that he can no longer harm her, now that they have been seen together. Perhaps that was why he wanted to meet her.

'Did you use your hands?' Celeste asks all of a sudden, intensely and very seriously.

'What did you say?' Heller asks. That really wasn't what he expected. Not yet.

'She trusted you, didn't she?'

'I don't know what you're talking about. I don't know why I'm sitting here listening to you,' he replies. And he feels terribly clumsy in this feeble attempt at self-defence.

Celeste looks past him, as though drawn to something in the street, beyond the café doorway.

'I want to see where you live,' she says.

'You want to see what?' Heller replies, confused. But he doesn't have time to ponder the question, because Celeste has already risen to her feet, picked up her backpack and jacket and headed for the door.

Hey, wait a moment, he wants to say. In fact that's exactly the phrase being acted out by his body as it lurches towards her, leaving him firmly behind.

Heller starts to follow her, then remembers that he still has to pay for his coffee; torn between the need to pay and his fear of losing her, he nervously peels the damp bill from beneath the saucer to take it over to the cashier.

With abrupt and hesitant gestures, and still craning his neck towards Celeste, who has already stepped into the street, he pays for his coffee under the puzzled gaze of the cashier and the barman. As he collects his change, he realises that he will never again visit this café as insouciantly as he has in the past.

When he finally leaves, he sees Celeste on the pavement opposite, entering the front door of his building.

He crosses the street, almost at a run.

'Excuse me, Miss!' bellows the porter as Celeste walks straight past his office.

She stops and turns around.

'She's with me,' Heller says.

'Oh, I'm sorry, Avvocato, I didn't see you,' he replies. He looks at Celeste, and then back at Heller, his respect for the latter suddenly diminished.

Two points, thinks Heller.

By the time he catches up with Celeste, she has already entered the lift, leaving the door open. As the lift ascends, she adjusts her bandana in the mirror, paying no attention to Heller, who stands uselessly beside her, thinking What on earth is she doing? Who is this girl? Why am I letting her into my home? realising that he is at least as dismayed by his own inability to react as by the ease with which she is making him do whatever she wants. He smells a faint hint of face powder, and although he is disturbed by this distracting thought, he is forced to acknowledge that she is beautiful, and reproaches himself for not having noticed that fact as they were sitting in the café.

The lift reaches his floor. Celeste opens the door and steps out in front of him.

'This way – or that?' she asks, pointing her index finger at the doors which face each other, one at either end of the corridor. An ordinary gesture, filled with intent. To which, incredibly, he responds. He finds himself going along with the girl's attitude as though it would be unreasonable to contradict her. As though he couldn't stop and say, Hang on a second. Where the hell do you think you're going? Who invited you in? And he is sufficiently self-aware to realise that he is not acting this way for fear of blackmail, which has not in any case been mentioned. There is something about her that prevents him from reacting in any coherent and concrete way, as though he wants to let her get on with it, to see her incomprehensible behaviour through to its conclusion. And all of this has happened in only a very short space of time, in the brief interval between the café and his building. And how everything has changed from the first moment he saw her.

He slips the key into the lock. He can't believe that this hand, the one that is opening his front door, really belongs to him.

Celeste lets him walk in, then follows. She puts her backpack on the floor. Her eyes wide open, she studies the walls around her as she hands her jacket to Heller, who receives it and hangs it on the coat-rack. Then she walks through the flat, down the long corridor in front of her.

'How high are these walls?' she asks.

'Four metres,' Heller replies.

'Four metres,' she repeats.

On her left, through the gap between two sliding panels of the doorway, she glimpses a library that occupies an entire wall.

'Your study?' she asks.

'Yes,' Heller replies with a hint of self-satisfaction.

Celeste walks in. She could have asked my permission, Heller thinks.

Celeste moves around the study as though she were a friend of his. The pleasant confusion of the papers and the files on the desk, the Post-it notes attached to the computer, the flashing light of the answering machine, a beautiful old painting (a riverbank baptism scene) on the only wall that is devoid of bookshelves, which otherwise dominate the space and give it a warm and lived-in air. Beneath the window is a white armchair, its arms worn and frayed, and in front of it an old radio serving as a coffee table. Or a footstool. Or both.

Heller stands in the doorway, waiting for something to happen.

'Lovely,' says Celeste, running a hand along the tops of the files lined up in the filing cabinet.

Irritated by the brazenness of her gesture, Heller pretends not to notice the compliment.

'Criminal negligence, is that the phrase?' says Celeste, walking towards the window.

Heller gives a start.

'In putative legitimate defence,' Celeste completes the phrase, accompanying herself with a finger as though reading a score.

So she was in court this morning. His workplace. The stage on which his life is played. She has seen him in his favourite suit. She has heard him speak. Argue. Defend. She knows more about him than she should.

'You're very good at being right,' she says. And she passes in front of him, leaving the room. Where's she off to now?

Heller watches her walk down the corridor; halfway, she turns.

'Is this where you did it?' she says abruptly. The same tone she used before, in the café.

Heller feels rage rising into his mouth. Finally he manages to react naturally. Snarling, he explodes from the doorway of his study. Celeste shields herself with her arms. Heller grips her by the throat anyway. He presses her against the wall. Celeste's face contracts in pain. Her heavy soles hit the wall, making a noise like a rattle of bones. She goes on protecting herself with her open palms, striking out impotently at the air, while he grips her arms tightly. Heller feels a genuine stab of pain. A profound remorse, an anguish that clutches at him just as he becomes aware of the beauty in the eyes in front of him. Celeste clings to his arms. She gasps for breath.

'Don't move,' he says.

She looks at him contemptuously. She clenches her teeth, then leans her head on one side and lets her hands fall to her thighs. Heller admires her courage. He moves his hands from her arms to her shoulders. Celeste feels his hands patting her chest, her back, her belt, her legs, between her legs, her shoes.

'Fine, you're not carrying anything,' says Heller, on his knees.

'What sort of anything? A gun, a knife, a razor, a microphone, what?' says Celeste defiantly.

Heller stands up. He feels his hands dangling uselessly at his sides. He doesn't know what to say.

'Let me past,' Celeste says, pushing him away with a forearm. And she heads furiously for the door.

Heller feels drained. He watches her back. Absurd as it may seem, he is ashamed of the search to which he has just subjected her. He catches up with her in the hall as she collects her jacket from the coat-rack and her backpack from the floor.

'Where's the little girl?' he says.

Celeste freezes by the door, as though the question were a knife in her back. She turns and looks at him with hostility and pain. Then she presses the handle down, opens the door and leaves.

14

At the end of the school day the playground is filled with the hubbub of Vespas revving and pulling off, shouted names, people jostling and craning their necks, faces scanning the multicoloured crowd for other faces that don't return their gaze. The traffic outside the gate, proceeding at a walking pace, seems further impeded by groups of young people spilling onto the street before dispersing along the pavement.

Celeste lingers with two girls from another class who are telling her about an oral exam that reached an unexpected conclusion. The story is told with great excitement, one girl correcting the other from time to time, as though she had been the only witness to the events.

The essence of the story was more or less as follows. Twice accused of incompetence for failing to understand a question, one of their classmates had turned his back on the teacher and returned to his desk beneath the teacher's startled gaze, saying, 'Ask somebody competent, then.'

'You should have seen the look on that bastard's face,' the less garrulous of the girls says, rather artificially, out of a need to add something of her own to the story so far monopolised by the other.

'Bloody right,' Celeste remarks smugly. And looking distractedly around, she becomes aware of the Great Dane sitting on the opposite pavement, so motionless that it looks like a life-sized ceramic model, an ornament outside a gift shop. Her lips part.

'What is it?' asks one of the girls.

Celeste stares transfixed. The other girl follows her gaze but can't see anything in particular.

'No, I just remembered something,' Celeste says, thoroughly distracted. 'Got to go.'

The girls glance at each other as Celeste leaves the playground and starts walking along the pavement, keeping her eye on the other side of the road.

The man is leaning against his double-parked car. He looks as though he's dressed for a date. Clean-shaven, a light suit, unbuttoned shirt, Franciscan sandals. He's waiting for her.

Celeste continues walking until she can look straight into the man's eyes, directly across the tarmac that separates them. The man gives her a crooked smile with a very clear message: I've come to get you. Then he beckons to her. The self-assurance of an animal trainer.

Celeste steps off the pavement and across the road; then, halfway, she stops. The man leans his head to one side, uncomprehending. A car hoots as it avoids Celeste, who still stands motionless in the middle of the road. The man moves instinctively, as though to walk towards her, his posture tense and ambiguous, caught between the need to keep her from being run over and the desire to impel her to obedience; and at this precise moment the terms of the encounter are reversed.

Just as the man moves away from the car, the dog follows him, responding to a conditioned reflex which makes it leap to attention the moment its master shifts position, keeping an eye on the area around him. Celeste reaches the far side of the road. Now they're standing face to face.

'Keep the dog away from me or I'm out of here,' Celeste orders.

The man frowns and gives a half-smile, pretending to be shocked by her tone. Then he stretches his arm out towards the Great Dane, which suddenly freezes and stares at its master as though enquiring whether it has understood correctly. Then the man wags his index finger in the air and the dog returns to stand where it had been.

'Happy now?' the man says with an evidently hypocritical sweetness. 'You see, I do whatever you want.'

'What the fuck are you doing here?' says Celeste furiously, staring at him.

'Will you come for a little drive with us?' he asks, ignoring her question. And he indicates the car with both hands, as though offering it to her as a present. 'I had it washed specially for you. We'll take the dog to the park, then get something to eat in this fantastic fish restaurant run by a friend of mine.'

Celeste says nothing.

'Wait,' says the man. 'I'll put the dog in the car, so you can stop worrying so much.'

The man opens the driver's door, pushes the seat forward and lets the Great Dane in. The dog stretches out on the whole of the back seat, its neck straight, like a real bodyguard. Then he shuts the door and waits for Celeste, who walks towards him.

'I'll leave him in the car, if you like, and we can go on foot.'

Celeste looks at the dog behind the window, then approaches the man. She looks him up and down, lingering over the opening of his shirt. He looks quizzically back at her. Celeste slowly raises her eyes, still concealing her intentions. Then, stretching her neck, she offers him her mouth.

'Never come anywhere near my school ever again,' says Celeste, brushing his lips with hers.

The man feels a slight stinging sensation, something distant that he can't quite place, uncertain whether it even has anything to do with him. Instinct precedes intellect, making him pull back his hand before he has time to register that that is precisely where the injury is.

Celeste takes a step backwards. The man looks at her, then at himself. There is a long, deep gash on the back of his hand, baring the flesh. The blood has reached his shirtsleeve, and shows no sign of stopping.

From inside the car the dog shows its fangs and snarls, then begins to bark. Standing fully upright, its head crashes violently against the roof of the car.

Fearing the man's reaction, Celeste retreats even

further. She holds the hand with the blade at her thigh.

The man bends his arm and holds it in the air, like someone who has just been asked to give a blood sample. He waves his other hand at random around the wound. His mouth is twisted into an ugly grimace, the cut seems to be giving him a lot of pain.

The dog is barking crazily, biting at the air, scratching the seats with its claws. Saliva sprays from its jaws, colliding stickily with the windows.

The man unbuttons his cuff and pulls it down as far as possible, drawing his hand back inside it to cover the wound.

The dog howls and crashes its head against the windows. The car rocks back and forth, and looks as though it might topple over at any moment.

'Fine,' says the man, with a meaningful sigh.

Without taking his eyes off her, he opens the driver's door. Immediately the Great Dane tries to leap out of the car to attack the enemy. The man stops it in mid-air, chopping it on the muzzle with a fist. A blow that hurls the animal backwards, forcing it to sit down on the back seat.

The man gets into the car, slams the door and turns on the ignition. The dog, confused by the incongruity of the orders and punishments it has received, yelps as it strikes its feet repeatedly against the fabric of the seat.

Celeste puts her hand in her pocket and walks away.

15

The Penal Section of the Palace of Justice manages to convey an oppressive sense of bleakness even at ten o'clock in the morning. The bulbs that barely produce any light (would it really be so hard to install brighter ones?); the decadence of the wood and marble fittings; the Fascist insignia etched on the office windows; the families of the defendants wandering between the courtrooms like patients in a hospital ward; the policemen along the corridors; the lawyers coming and going with all their props, wrapped up in their gowns and wearing dyspeptic facial expressions; the normality acted out by one and all, as though they weren't all in a place of condemnation and punishment, each playing its part in the collective representation of guilt.

His gown folded over his arm, Heller wanders the corridors as he waits for his case to be called. His mind feels fresh because, strangely enough, he has actually slept for the first time in days. Deeply, uninterruptedly and, as far as he can remember, without dreams or any kind of disturbance. He is still sceptical of this feeling of serenity and, suspecting that it might be a collateral effect of his anxiety, a joke played on him by fear, he remains on the defensive.

When the girl went away, he left the flat and walked the pavements for a long time, memorising and focusing on every single detail of their encounter, analysing his fresh memories for fear that they might fade. He scrutinised the girl's behaviour and his own, first separately, and then in relation to each other. He walked halfway around the city to finish his meticulous task of memory. Then he went back home, slipping into that blissful sleep he had not experienced for so long.

And now that the reconstruction of events is filed away in his clear mind, he is able to reflect on his situation schematically, as he would normally tend to do.

Thus he believes he can separate the girl's behaviour into two stages so different as to contradict one another: firstly, running from the initial phone calls to the meeting in the café, reveals calculation and cold determination in the pursuit of a goal; the other, essentially the time spent in his flat, is the stage that is ambiguous and inconclusive.

As for the first of these, he is particularly struck by the effectiveness of the pretext with which the girl tricked and wrong-footed him, before drawing him into a public place in which her safety would be assured once they had been seen together. It was a clear sequence of carefully planned moves, a cool ability to compress and coalesce times and distances as a way of working on her opponent's anxiety and taking advantage of his impulsive reactions: had the café been even so much as a block away, rather than just below his flat, Heller – he is well aware – would not have been so quick to agree to a meeting; had the girl postponed the appointment by as little as half an hour, he would certainly have used that margin to prepare some kind of a counter-strategy.

In the second stage, on the other hand, the plot begins to collapse. There is no request, no blackmail is forthcoming, there is no sign of any potential outcome. The girl (and, incidentally, he doesn't even know her name) becomes distant, closes herself impenetrably away. When Heller attempts to question her, he seems to provoke a highly personal feeling of resentment in her.

This second type of behaviour is all the more disconcerting in that it blatantly abandons the successes of the first, leaving unfinished a promising process that could easily have achieved its goal. And it is here that Heller's logic fails him. Because even if he tries to think of the girl as an enemy against whom he must defend himself, he is forced to admit to himself that what he feels for her is not distaste, not suspicion, but rather a desire to know her, a cautious form of trust.

He recalls her brief and disturbing phrases, her terrifying self-possession as she walked around his flat, those questions that came from nowhere. If he concentrates a little, he can just hear that little voice speaking to him.

Then he starts reasoning as a lawyer again. He repeats to himself that the serious risk he thought he ran is now reduced to a little girl who says she knows. *Says* she knows. And she has no proof, because there can't be anything left. To see his flat: that was all she asked.

At that moment the hypothesis of a possible police operation inevitably comes to his mind. Heller considers it, weighs it up, rejects it. Of all those possibilities, the idea of a decoy dispatched in search of clues is the one that convinces him least. And he frisked her himself. She wasn't carrying anything.

So?

'Avvocato,' calls a prisoner being escorted by two policemen as they pass close by him. Heller nods with little conviction. Then a name suddenly springs to mind.

Vincenzo Rubicondo. No, Vinicio.

When he defended this man at least ten years before, he was little more than a boy. Look at him now, taller than the policemen walking beside him. They had caught him and two stupid mates of his stealing a car radio. After the trial he had turned up at Heller's flat full of gratitude, with 200,000 lira and a can of Coke.

Heller has never again received a fee of that kind, throughout the whole of his career. It still gives him pleasure to remember it.

It's nice when your former clients greet you.

Later, he might even pop round to the courtroom to which they're taking the man, and find out what he's been up to this time.

Heller continues to pace the corridors, waiting for the bailiff to leave the courtroom and give him some idea of when his case is going to come up. His back is bent slightly, his forehead creased in a frown. His hands behind his back, he rotates his thumbs around each other.

Especially when wearing his gown, he often finds himself adopting certain poses that he realises he must have acquired unconsciously. Then he straightens his back and touches his hair, partly to check that he still has some.

The sight of a familiar female face interrupts his thoughts. She must be about ten metres away. She's talking into her mobile, walking around aimlessly in the middle of the corridor. Her hair is down, a bit shorter than he remembers, a loose sweater, corduroy trousers and boots. A studiedly casual look.

Heller is spellbound. Seeing her so close, and all of her at once, both her unique and unmistakeable body and the particular syntax of its motion through space, causes him an unidentifiable pain.

Busy as she is with the tiny gadget, which gives her the disconcerting freedom of simultaneously talking on the phone while at the same time going wherever she wants (an intrinsically illogical possibility, she insists), Elena Cassinari doesn't immediately register Heller's face. Then, as she continues to move about randomly, her eyes catch his, and the thing in her hand becomes a useless piece of plastic. The person at the other end goes on talking for a while, before noticing that no one is listening.

Heller stays put. He may be smiling at her.

She waits for him for a few long minutes. Then she lowers her head, and it is as though an invisible beam runs directly from her to him, running along the middle of the floor before filling his body from bottom to top.

Heller stands there, disconcerted and unable to act,

softened by an unhappiness the cause of which he can't identify.

And he wonders whether, from that distance, Elena can sense this.

But it doesn't matter much, because when he finally musters the strength to turn around and walk in the opposite direction, he feels as if he is walking with the slowness of renunciation.

'Ah, Mr Heller,' says a voice right behind his head.

Heller turns. It is the magistrate who was acting as public prosecutor in the farmer's trial. He is leaving the Court of Appeal, caught between his haste to be else-where and the temptation to linger for at least a moment with Heller, as though he has something to give him.

'Greetings,' says Heller, sniffing conflict in the air.

The magistrate is careful not to shake his hand, a detail that Heller notices immediately.

'I wanted to tell you that I liked the issue of excessive force. In legitimate defence – what was it? Putative, that's it, yes,' he says, in a tone so ironic that it brings a vaguely insane gleam to his eye. 'Truly imaginative,' he adds. And as he prepares to leave he looks Heller in the face, searching for an embarrassment that he fails to find. Then he perseveres: 'For a moment I was worried that you were going to set up an opposition between malice and negligence, that you were going to come up with virtual homicide or something of the kind.'

Heller allows a very brief silence before he replies, with great composure.

'You have a great line in jokes. I've been told that you're a very funny guy.'

The magistrate blushes visibly. His features harden into an expression of modest sincerity. That's what he must have been like as a child, Heller thinks.

'But he'll lose on appeal, Heller. Don't you worry.'

'Could be. But I've won for the time being.'

The magistrate compresses his lips. Behind him, a tiny man pops out of one of the courtrooms and looks around.

'Avvocato Heller!'

Heller rises on tiptoe to peer over the dumbstruck face of the man in front of him, and nods to the bailiff calling from the doorway to let him know that it is his turn.

'Excuse me,' says Heller. And he walks around the magistrate, who stands irresolutely on the spot.

As he makes his way towards the courtroom, he is tempted to turn back and say, Weren't you in a hurry?

But then he decides not to bother.

It's four o'clock when the entryphone rings in his study. Heller goes and picks it up.

'Avvocato?' the porter asks.

'Yes,' he says, already prepared.

'There's a visitor here to see you, the same girl as yesterday.'

The same girl as yesterday. Some phrases are so judgemental that people should be ashamed to pronounce them.

'Send her up.'

He opens the door, leaves it ajar, goes back into his study and sits down at the desk. He inspects the library in front of him. He counts the volumes of law reports, then runs his eye along the files on display. Ah, yes Saraceno, he thinks, picking up a file at random. The case is going to be heard on Friday week, if I remember correctly. He should get probation.

The sound of the lift stopping at his floor. The doors sliding open. Footsteps on the landing. The door to his flat. The click of the closing door. The thump of those heavy soles.

'Hi,' says Celeste in the doorway.

'What brings you back?' Heller asks, turning round.

Celeste enters, drops the backpack on one of the two chairs reserved for his clients, takes off her jacket and drops it on the desk, ignoring the file lying open there.

Heller looks at the jacket, then at her.

'Oh, sorry,' says Celeste. And picking it up from the desk she puts it on the chair, next to the backpack.

'I like your study,' she says, removing the bandana from her hair and tying it around her wrist.

'Yes,' says Heller, 'you've said that before.'

And he stares at the backpack from the other side of the desk.

Celeste walks along the bookshelves, running her finger carelessly along the spines of the law books one by one. She reaches the armchair beneath the window and sits down. She looks at the old radio in front of her, then at Heller.

'Can I put my feet on it?' she asks.

'First get that backpack off there,' he says, 'or I'll turn it upside down and shake it.'

'What, are you going to frisk me again?'

Heller doesn't reply.

Celeste gets to her feet, walks past the desk and leaves the study. Heller stays where he is. A moment later he hears the squeak of a cupboard door and the sound of a tap running. He gets up and goes into the kitchen.

Celeste is filling a glass of water. Heller stops in the doorway. She ignores him. She drinks and puts the glass back in the cupboard without rinsing it. Heller follows this performance with his head cocked, as though unable to believe that the scene he is witnessing is actually being played out in his kitchen.

By the window a budgie's cage hangs from an iron ring attached to the end of a microphone stand. Celeste walks over to it, intrigued. The bird suddenly jumps from its central perch to the trapeze in the top corner of the cage, moving its head in tiny jerks.

'What a strange thing,' Celeste says, running her hand along the stand. 'But I like it,' she says triumphantly, turning towards Heller. And then she immediately returns to her new discovery. 'How long have you had it?' she asks, leaning down to bring herself level with the cage, stooping low, her hands on her knees.

'A few years, I guess,' Heller replies, startled by the relaxed way in which she turns her back on him.

'What's its name?' Celeste asks. And she follows the bird as it jumps from the trapeze to the bars of the cage and remains there, fluttering its wings to maintain its precarious balance, anticipating the movements of the stranger looming over its home.

'It doesn't have a name,' says Heller irritably. 'It isn't a dog, what's it going to do with a name?'

Celeste lets the words fade away in the silence of the room, then continues.

'How come it doesn't sing?'

'Pff. It never has.'

'What is it, dumb?'

'How should I know?'

'Well, it is yours. You ought to know.'

'Well I don't.'

Celeste looks all around the cage. Meanwhile the budgerigar has moved to the bottom, where it is hopping up and down in confusion. All of a sudden Heller finds the girl's behaviour frankly intolerable. And as though she has heard him say so, she continues: 'Its water's dirty.'

'I don't think so.'

'What do you mean you don't think so? It's yellow!'

Heller is beginning to get riled; then, as if coming to his senses, he is angry that he has allowed himself to be dragged into this kind of conversation. What on earth am I doing? he thinks. Why am I answering these stupid questions?

'The water's dirty. And the cage is dirty too,' she insists.

'That's not true. It gets cleaned every day, for heaven's sake.'

And just to make his point, he opens the cage door (the

budgerigar flies madly along the edge of the roof), removes the water dish, pulls it out and closes the door. Then he goes to the sink, turns on the tap, carefully rinses the dish, fills it and returns to the cage to put it back.

At that moment Heller finds himself thinking that he could kill her. An idea that settles in his mind like a leaf on a lawn. Without conflict, trauma or rage. He knows it would be an act of genuine madness; that the porter recognised her and let her in; that by now several witnesses have seen them together; that she might have talked to someone or left clues that would lead straight to him if she were suddenly to disappear; and yet at that point he would be willing to ignore each of these valid reasons and walk round the table, grip her head between his hands and take her life without a struggle or a drop of blood, in little more than a moment.

He moves to the doorway, considering the negligible distance that separates the scene in his mind from the gesture that he does not make, thinking about how quickly the criminal thought comes to life before crashing into action. Then he becomes aware that Celeste is staring at him.

'You're thinking about it too much,' she says.

Heller opens his eyes wide.

'About what?'

Celeste doesn't reply immediately.

'About me.'

'What are you talking about?' says Heller, his voice dropping suddenly to a whisper.

Celeste walks to him. She folds her arms over her

belly, grips her pullover at hip level, and pulls it over her head in a rotating motion that lingers in the air for a few seconds.

Heller follows her confident movements uneasily. When he begins to understand what they mean, he feels as if he is going to faint.

Celeste drops the pullover on the table. Then she takes off her white t-shirt, revealing her bony shoulders and her small, pale breasts, for the first time giving off the smell of naked flesh.

'This is how you do it, isn't it?'

'Get your clothes back on, I don't know what you're talking about,' says Heller.

'Come on,' she presses him.

Heller shrinks back.

'I didn't do what you think I did.'

'Why, what do I think you did?' she asks, stepping closer to him.

Heller holds onto the back of a chair. I don't like little girls, he wants to say, but realises that it would sound meaningless. His head spins.

Celeste talks to him in such a low voice that he can hardly hear her.

'You can only do it by stealth. If I trusted you, then you could. If I wasn't expecting it, then you could.'

Heller pushes her away with a hand, feeling a sudden wave of nausea that nearly knocks him over. How does she know these things? he thinks.

'Please stop, that's enough,' he says, finally sitting down.

Celeste slips her jumper back on. She leaves the kitchen. Heller remains seated where he is, with his hands on the table, watching the budgerigar in the cave hopping back and forth as if asking him for an explanation.

A few minutes later he hears the sound of the television. He gets to his feet, leaves the kitchen, sleepwalks his way down the corridor and appears in the sitting room.

Celeste is sitting on the sofa, the remote control in her hand, flicking from one channel to another.

Heller stands motionless for a second, then returns to the study. He sits down at the desk and stares absently at the books around him as though somehow detached from himself and from any physical object. He actually finds it quite pleasant.

After a while the television falls silent. Heller hears the unmistakeable sound of those shoes along the corridor.

Celeste enters and picks up her backpack and her jacket from the chair where she left them. As she does so, she spots a stone paperweight on the desk, roughly oval in shape, very pale, run through with blue veins.

'Lovely,' she says.

Heller still can't bring himself to look her in the face.

'I like stones. Who gave it to you?'

'No one, I found it.'

'Where?'

'In the sea, as a boy, a long way out, where the rocks end and the seaweed begins.'

'I want it,' she says.

'I'm really fond of it. It's something I've had for many years, it reminds me of my childhood.'

'Give it to me,' says Celeste. And without waiting for his reply, she picks it up from the surface of the desk and starts to slip it into the inside pocket of her backpack.

Heller looks at his stone, which is leaving him to go and belong to someone else, and he thinks absurdly about the summer when he found it, his fear of swimming so far out, and the friends he played with: he remembers their names, their faces and the towns they came from, he remembers the voice of the lifeguard, the wooden jetty that led down to the sea, the swimming pool full of sulphurous water, where the heads of adults could be seen bobbing about, diving, or standing talking in low voices; he is unhappy, very unhappy, that from now on he won't see the stone on his desk, and with a surge of regret he says goodbye to it as the girl's hands close the clasp of the backpack pocket, taking it away for ever.

'I'll be back tomorrow,' says Celeste.

Heller sits there until he hears the door close. When Celeste's footsteps begin to echo down the stairs he gets up, takes his jacket off the back of the armchair and hurries out too.

16

The late morning sun beats hard upon the concrete square in front of the entrance to the prison. David Heller, wearing dark glasses and clutching his briefcase, passes a large group of prisoners' relatives waiting by the gate, carrying shopping bags. He takes off his sunglasses to show his face on the video entryphone monitor, and presses the button. The luminous peephole above the steel panel comes on almost immediately, and his face fills the screen.

'Move back,' a voice says slowly through the loud-speaker.

Heller steps backwards and moves his head so that his face is in the middle of the monitor.

'Ah, Avvocato,' says the same voice, in a completely different tone.

The gate lock opens electronically. Heller begins to pass through the gate, and is immediately followed by some of the visiting relatives, trying to slip in behind him.

'Not you lot!' commands the voice from the loudspeaker. 'We'll let you know when you can come in.'

Heller crosses the internal courtyard, holding his hand as a visor to shield his eyes against the bright sun. At the reception, a guard in his shirtsleeves, decidedly overweight and younger than he looks, greets him like an old friend.

'We haven't seen you for a long time, Mr Heller.'

'Not that long,' says Heller, walking over to the window of the small elevated office and taking his pen from his breast pocket. 'About three weeks, or a little more. It's just that time stands still in here, even for you.'

'You're right there,' observes the prison officer, opening his visitor register and turning it towards Heller. 'And every now and again these guys get out, while we're stuck inside.'

Heller signs the register and writes the name of the prisoner he wants to meet.

'Ah, yes. He's working in the accounts office now. I'll have someone take you to him right away,' says the guard, struggling up from his chair. And he calls out to another prison officer, assigning him the task of escorting the lawyer to the visiting room.

A few minutes later, Heller is strolling around a room that looks very like a cell (there's even a tap in one corner), furnished with a slightly battered office desk, two chairs and a bench against one wall.

Visiting room, he thinks, looking at the long slit that runs along the top of one wall, just below the ceiling, just wide enough to let in a weak, yellowish light.

The door opens. Heller's client enters, wearing a tracksuit and bomber jacket, visibly surprised.

'How are you?' says Heller, extending a hand.

The man shakes it and continues looking at him quizzically as he sits down on the other side of the desk.

'I'm well, Mr Heller. But what are you doing here?'

'I just felt like it. How are things with you?'

'What do you think? I'm here,' he says with a shrug.

'True. But I'll get you out soon, you'll see.'

Heller's client studies his face as if it's covered with spots.

'So what's going on, Mr Heller, has something happened?'

'Something? Oh, with your trial you mean? No, no news there.'

'Ah. I was worried,' the man replies, assuming a more relaxed expression and resting his elbows on the surface of the desk.

'Sure,' observes Heller. Then he gazes vacantly into the middle distance.

'So what've you come here to ask me about?'

'You know,' Heller improvises, speaking thickly, 'sometimes you find yourself in strange situations, and you don't know how to act.'

That's what he says.

And this is what he is thinking: If I trusted you, then you could. If I wasn't expecting it, then you could.

The client leans forwards, bringing his face closer to Heller's.

The lawyer is growing less sure about the favour he had been planning to ask this man when, already far from convinced, he got into the car to go to the prison, hoping to decide along the way. And he continues hesitantly, as though talking, even about nothing, might help him get to the point.

'I don't know if you've ever found yourself in a dilemma you want to get out of, and you can't. You know, when you're sure that something's about to happen but you don't talk to anyone about it because nobody would understand.'

At this point Heller stops, embarrassed by the indecisive image of himself that he is presenting, and he feels as though he is watching his own scrambled sentences reassembling themselves in the staring face of his client – who breaks the silence with a hurried question.

'This dilemma you can't get out of, has it got a first and a second name?'

Heller looks at the slit of light below the ceiling. He doesn't reply.

'Mr Heller, give me a cigarette, please.'

'A cigarette?'

'Yeah, a cigarette. Have you got any?'

'Of course,' Heller replies. And he takes a half-full pack from his inside jacket pocket. The client glances towards the door, reaches towards him and takes the pack from his hand. Then, bringing thumb and index finger together, he mimes in the air the act of writing.

Heller does as he suggests, although without understanding: he takes his pen from his breast pocket, unscrews the cap and hands it to his client. The man takes it, darts another glance at the door, quickly writes something on the inside of the top of the pack, and hands it back to Heller.

'Listen to me. You must have a reason for coming here. Don't worry about a thing, let me do it.'

'No, forget it, don't give me any advice, I just came to say hello.'

His client dismisses his words with a wink.

'When you've made your decision, send us a smoke signal. You just have to mention my name. Anything you need.'

'Yes, fine. Thanks,' says Heller, almost leaping to his feet, as though the conversation has reached a line he doesn't want to cross. He picks up his bag and walks to the door, so confused that he forgets to shake hands with his client, who calls to him from inside:

'Avvocato?'

Heller turns round, startled.

'Anything.'

Leaving the prison, Heller holds his briefcase as a shield against the sun. As always when he leaves this place, he is struck by the sudden increase in temperature which makes him feel slightly dizzy.

Prisons really are cold places. It must be the thick walls.

There are no relatives waiting outside now. Heller collects his vehicle from the car park, takes off his jacket, unbuttons his cuffs and sets off.

He drives with his arm out the window, looking every now and again into the rear-view mirror, not entirely convinced that expressing his gratitude will be such an easy matter. He drives slowly, dazed and somehow tainted by the meeting that has just taken place.

So now he's done this, too.

He checks the time. 'I'll be back tomorrow,' the girl said as she took his stone.

Heller doesn't like waiting at home. And he has no desire to go back there, not right now. Anyway, it's a lovely day. He'll catch a bite to eat on the way.

He takes the coast road and stops at the first restaurant he comes to. The kind with tables outside and a car park covered by a dense roof of woven rushes, above it a sign reading 'Nothing But Freshness', whatever that means.

Heller sits down with his back to the sea and looks at the road. He orders some pasta and a bottle of water. A light breeze has risen, it's fairly quiet (just a car every now and again), and the light puts a slight strain on his eyes. As he sits there dazed in those drearily relaxing surroundings, he starts feeling like a normal person again.

A voice suddenly rouses him.

'Do you want this key ring?'

Heller opens his eyes and sees a girl standing in front of him. She's about four foot nine, with long, gleaming chestnut hair that contrasts with her dirty skin. She is wearing a yellow sweatshirt, a size too small for her, and a skirt with horizontal coloured stripes that looks rather like a parasol. She has no shoes, just sagging, thick woollen socks. She is smiling broadly. Heller has never seen a Gypsy with such straight teeth.

'Hey, I asked you a question.'

'Sorry, I was distracted.'

'Well?' says the girl, pointing at the key ring on the table. A soft rubber hedgehog tied to a piece of string with a ring at the end.

'Ah. Yes, why not,' says Heller. And he begins to take his wallet out of the inside pocket of his jacket. 'Have you eaten?' he asks.

'What did you say?' the girl says, surprised.

'I asked you if you'd eaten.'

'Yes, I've eaten,' she replies, even more baffled than before.

'Fine,' says Heller. 'How much is the key ring?'

'Two euros,' she says.

'Really,' replies Heller. And he takes a ten-euro note from his wallet.

'I've got no change,' says the girl.

'I don't want any,' he says. 'But I'll only give you the money if you keep it.'

'Why?'

'Because I know how this works. You go home and they take everything you've earned.'

'No, no,' she says, firmly shaking her head. 'I know what I want to buy.'

'Really?' Heller seems very interested. 'What would that be?'

'A dress. Lovely. Long. With flowers. I measured it two days ago, at the market.'

'That sounds great. So look, we'll do it this way,' he says, rising slightly from his chair so as to slip a hand into his trouser pocket. 'I'll give you the two euros for the key ring, so that you can show them you've sold it, and you keep the ten.'

The girl takes the coin that Heller hands her, looks at it, then back at him.

Heller smiles at her.

'What's your name?' he asks her.

'Varika,' says the girl. 'What about you?'

'Dario,' Heller replies.

The girl bites her lower lip. She seems to feel an intense need to give him something in return.

'Then I'll show you the dress.'

'I'd love that,' says Heller. 'But who knows whether we'll ever meet again?'

'I'm always here,' she says, sweeping the air with her arm to indicate the stretch of coastline.

Heller can barely conceal his excitement.

A little over an hour later, on this same road, not more than a kilometre away, a car brakes violently.

There is a man in the car, and a Great Dane on the back seat.

The man opens the door and leaps out at Celeste, his eyes filled with a terrible euphoria.

Here we go, she thinks, as she stands and waits.

Perhaps because there's no point in running, he'd catch her anyway.

Or perhaps, more simply, because she doesn't want to.

17

'It's out of order!' the porter warns, emerging from his office as, pointlessly, Celeste continues to press the button of the lift which refuses to come.

Heller has already opened his door, and is waiting for her in the study as usual, preparing to conceal his emotion as best he can. Yesterday he realised at precisely four-thirty that she wasn't coming. He was busy preparing a prison release application when his eye, not entirely by chance, wandered over to the clock on the wall, and he was blinded by the overwhelming realisation that he was waiting for the girl with every molecule of his being; and every movement he had made, everything he had done over the last few hours, from that unsettling exchange at the jail to the lunch by the sea, and finally the legal opinion that he was writing at that moment, was nothing but a series of distractions, expedients designed to pass the time until her arrival.

At first he tried to ignore the dismay that this discovery had caused him. But the longer the afternoon dragged on without the buzz of the entryphone, the more significant her absence became.

And now that she's coming back at last, Heller succumbs to a feeling of relief, of gratitude, which makes him feel better while requiring no sacrifice on his part.

Clutching the banisters, Celeste drags herself up the stairs, one foot behind the other, like an old woman. It gets slightly easier between one step and the next. It's when she bends over, even a little, that it hurts.

Heller has been shivering for some time. He knows the lift is broken, but he still wonders why the girl is taking so long. When he hears the door close, he struggles to regain his composure, and waits.

A few long minutes pass, and still she doesn't appear, and still there is no sound of her. Heller gets to his feet and steps out of the room to look towards his front door.

And there she is. Leaning with her back to the wall, though. As if she can't walk.

'What's wrong?' he asks.

All of a sudden Celeste opens her eyes wide, and abruptly assumes a different posture. The effort is clearly very painful.

'I'm a bit out of breath,' she says.

Out of breath? Heller thinks. When it's taken you a quarter of an hour to climb the stairs?

Celeste comes towards him, trying to keep her mouth still.

'Are you sure you're OK?' says Heller, stepping back to let her into his study.

She nods, not overly concerned about whether he believes her or not. She shrugs off her backpack and lets it slide to the floor, takes off her jacket and hangs it over the back of one of the chairs intended for clients. Then she goes and sits in the armchair, beneath the window.

'You sat there last time, too,' Heller observes.

'I like corners,' she replies.

A brief, weighted silence follows, betraying Heller's need to change the subject.

'Why didn't you come?' he asks her finally, with obvious unease.

It's as though she hasn't heard him. She stretches her hands out between her legs and rubs them together. Then she gives a sort of smile, and turns to face the window.

'I saw you the other day,' she says.

'What?' asks Heller, who has understood very clearly.

'I can tell you the exact time, and the headlines of the newspaper you used to cover your face when I passed you.'

Heller thinks his mouth is half open and, what is worse, he feels it won't be easy to shut it.

'I know your car,' says Celeste.

Only then does she turn towards him.

One emotion that Heller thought he would never again experience is that of shame. That feeling that thickens the blood, makes you blush and destroys any sense of self.

Celeste, touched by Heller's unexpected display of vulnerability, rewards him with words that seem entirely sincere.

'You know, I liked seeing you, even if you were hiding.'

Heller wants to smile.

Celeste starts to get up, as though the conversation

had made her want to move; but she is caught by a violent, acid pain in her belly, which makes her sit back down. She brings a hand to her stomach, which is twisting in a series of little spasms that seem to follow a spiral path traced by the pain until it passes through her. Biting her lower lip, she holds her breath till the tension in her face has relaxed, giving way to an expression of dejection.

Heller hurries towards her, falling to his knees. He surrounds her with useless hands that don't even know whether or how to touch her.

'What's wrong, are you ill?'

'It's nothing.'

'What do you mean, it's nothing? You can't even move.'

'Would you give over? I told you, there's nothing wrong with me!' Celeste explodes, pushing him away.

Heller nearly falls backwards.

Celeste's face crumples into anger. With the pain, because it is coming back. With herself, for reacting as she has.

She snorts and struggles painfully to her feet.

'Fine, you really want to know? OK, take a look.'

And lifting her jumper to just below her breasts, she reveals two multicoloured bruises located a short distance from each other, between her ribs and navel. The higher of the two seems to pulse, as though a parasite were nestling beneath her skin.

Heller presses his lips together.

'Who did that to you?'

'It doesn't matter.'

'Christ almighty, why?'

'Why what?' she says stiffly.

Heller looks at her with embarrassment, already regretting the question.

'Why do I put myself in these situations? Why do I do it?'

Heller lowers his head, already acknowledging the worthlessness of any observation he might be able to come up with.

'No.'

'Oh. Fine,' says Celeste. And she sits down again.

A listless, drained sensation, the suspicion of being entirely useless. Heller backs away to his desk, and slides onto one of the clients' chairs.

'Tell me who it was. Tell me,' he asks her.

'I don't give a fuck about anything he can do to me,' says Celeste, as though she hadn't heard him.

Heller walks slowly over to her. He crouches down and runs a hand along an arm of the chair.

'Show me those bruises again, please.'

'Why?'

'Please.'

Celeste gets to her feet. Once again she lifts the jumper to her breasts, carefully keeping them covered. Looking down, she sees Heller's face, almost pressed against her belly. She feels as though the tenderness of her swollen flesh is amplified by the proximity of lips that want to touch her.

Heller's mouth settles on the larger of the two bruises.

Celeste shuts her eyes and bites her lip. With little twitches of her head she follows the intense and slightly painful sensation of that contact. Heller moves with the hunger of a nursing baby. With her free hand, Celeste grips his head and presses it to her, from an instinctive need to regulate the pressure of his lips.

'Tell me who it was,' says Heller.

She shakes her head, keeping her eyes closed.

Heller repeats the question until he gets an answer that gives him a clue. Then, in a sequence of questions like those in a police inquiry, questions designed to make a subsequent reconstruction possible, he asks her to describe her attacker, first briefly, and then in greater detail.

Still gripping his head with her hand, Celeste tells him everything, deriving a strange pleasure from her narrative, toying with his hatred.

At just about the same time, in a picturesque grove of holm oaks, just outside the city, the activists of a well-known environmental group, which consistently appears in the regional register of voluntary organisations, were liberating a buzzard and a kestrel, applauded by thirty-five children from three different secondary-school classes, accompanied by their teachers.

After refreshments of orange juice and organic honey cakes, the association's volunteers invited the children to go for a walk through the wood. Two of them, Massimo Cantalupo and Vincenzo Venuti, both twelve years old, and neither noted for their application or discipline,

146

wandered away from the group and plunged deeper into the wood, ignoring the calls of their teachers.

The following day, the initials MC and VV appeared on the front page of the local newspaper as those of the schoolchildren who had, during a nature ramble, found lying in a hole not far from a waterfall, covered by a slimy layer of branches and leaves, the corpse of a girl in an advanced state of decomposition. Still legible on her chest was a name, written in indelible ink.

18

You can tell right away when it's a stranger ringing the doorbell. It's like a question mark, the suspicion, groundless yet entirely natural, that you might be beholden to someone, the vague sense that they might have a legitimate claim against you.

David Heller is in his vest, his face covered with foam and a towel over his shoulders like a scarf, when he hears the bell and comes to just this conclusion. He puts his soapy shaving brush on the edge of the basin and heads for the door, quickening his pace in time with the insistent ringing.

'Coming!'

He opens the door. On the landing there is a woman of about fifty, evidently agitated. She is respectably dressed, clutching the handles of a handbag with both hands. Her slightly dishevelled hair suggests stress rather than negligence.

'Are you . . .' she says, her eye darting from Heller to the nameplate, as though the man who has appeared in front of her doesn't correspond to the professional figure announced on the door, '. . . Avvocato David Heller?'

Heller rubs his vest with his right hand, over his chest.

'Yes, why?'

'I'm Celeste's mother. Let me come in.'

As that name explodes in his head, scattering its syllables in all directions, Heller steps aside, obeying the woman's order without even registering the fact. He immediately realises why the woman looked familiar when he opened the door.

'Can I take your bag?' he asks, half closing the door.

'Too late for manners,' she snaps. 'I've come to warn you.'

'Warn me?'

The woman looks around as though she has never seen white walls before.

'So this is the library my daughter's been visiting,' she says with acid irony.

Heller shuts the door and says nothing, still startled by the woman's intrusion. She looks him up and down contemptuously, slippers to hair and back again. Heller is slightly embarrassed by how little he is wearing; he hadn't been expecting anyone, least of all a furious mother.

'You're a lawyer, a respectable person. You've got a lovely flat, and you're young. Aren't you ashamed of yourself?'

Heller looks down at himself, then at the woman.

'Excuse me, madam, but that's quite enough. I don't know you, I've never seen you before this moment. You turn up out of the blue, you ring my bell, you come into my house, you insult me. Calm down, now, and tell me what you want, or I'll throw you out.'

'So you can be boorish, too. It doesn't suit you.'

'Oh for God's sake,' says Heller, finding the situation suddenly ridiculous. 'If you don't stop this at once I'm going to have to call the police.'

'Fine, you just go and call them, so you can tell them yourself.'

'Tell them what?'

'That you're having sex with a minor.'

'That I'm—'

'Don't you try to be clever with me, I am very well aware that my daughter comes here every afternoon,' the woman breaks in, sitting down on the little sofa by the front door, as though taking possession of all the time and space she needs to deal with the subject at hand. A gesture that immediately makes Heller think of the reading of the indictment at the opening of a trial. He takes a breath, exhales through his nostrils, and looks as though he's deflating.

'You're wrong, madam.'

'Are you denying what I say?'

'Not what you say, but what you think. There's nothing going on between me and your daughter.'

'Oh, really? And I'm supposed to believe you?'

'It's the truth.'

'So why does Celeste come here? Why does she see you?'

I don't know, is what Heller should say, quite simply. It would be the truth, but would send the girl's mother into a fury, so he says nothing.

The funny thing is that while he feels frustrated by his

inability to release the woman before him from the suspicion that is tormenting her, he continues to study her
face and hands with an intense need to see in her a
resemblance to her daughter, a resemblance that
becomes more apparent, more sharply defined as she
moves and speaks.

The woman suddenly leaps to her feet, her suspicions
only confirmed by Heller's silence.

'I'm warning you,' she says, clumsily pointing a finger
at him as she presses down the door handle with her
other hand. 'Leave my daughter alone. Break off all
contact with her or I'll report you. I'll get you into real
trouble. I'll see to it that you end up on the street.'

'You're mistaken, madam, believe me,' Heller says to
her back.

On the landing, she turns around.

'And not a word to Celeste about this meeting. Do as
I say or I'll ruin you. Do you get that?'

'I repeat. Listen to me. You're mistaken,' Heller insists
stupidly, appearing at the banisters as the sound of the
woman's heels fades away down the stairs.

He remains on the landing until he hears a door
opening on the upper floor. Then he turns back inside
and prepares to go out, as he had been planning to.

Half an hour later he leaves a shop near his home with
a bag of chocolate eggs. Then he takes his car to make
another purchase in a large pet shop on the other side of
the city.

When he is done he heads towards the coast, driving
slowly and repeating the name in his head like someone

repeating a number he fears he might forget as he impatiently stamps his feet outside an occupied phone box.

He drives past her pitch. Even if she isn't there, he derives some comfort from seeing the advertisement on the car-park roof.

He pulls up without turning off the engine, in part to play the role of someone waiting for only a short time, and in part to remain in a place which, at that moment, gives him a sense of proximity to the girl.

At first he pays little heed to the Great Dane locked in a car that is parked a short distance away. Then, as though a skilful hand had gripped his head to turn it in that direction, he concentrates all his attention on the sight of the imprisoned animal, and inspects the surrounding area in the absolute conviction that he will soon locate the man he is looking for.

And there he is, on the pavement opposite, talking to a young boy on a Vespa. Couldn't be easier to spot, with that red hair, that red skin. And the dog. Really couldn't.

Handed to me on a plate, thinks Heller. Pathetic little creep. And he gets out of the car, seized by an irrepressible desire to be seen. He shuts the door, leans back against the bodywork and starts to stare at the man.

The man is still talking to the boy when he catches Heller's eye. He breaks off so suddenly that the boy turns round. The man dismisses him with a slap on the shoulder. As the boy switches on the ignition of his

Vespa and drives off, the man lowers his hands to his sides and stares back at Heller. Their tense exchange of glares lasts a few seconds, before being interrupted by the siren of an ambulance that has just turned into the road. Heller gets into his car and drives off. As he does so, he looks in his rear-view mirror, and the man watches him as he leaves.

Leaning against a metal pole, Celeste's mother returns home on the metro with the feeling of defeat that comes from pushing yourself too far. Although far from proud of what she has done, she confirms how successful it was by meticulously reconstructing every detail of her conversation with Heller, and in the fresh memory of his embarrassed reactions she realises how precise and effective her accusations were.

Before going home, she stops at the supermarket to buy something for dinner. As she hangs up her overcoat in the hall cupboard and walks towards the dining room with the shopping bags, she is comforted by the smell of home.

She has a curious feeling, as though her brain has somehow become stuck and she doesn't know what to tell her body to do, when she sees her husband sitting on the floor in the middle of the room, his legs outstretched and a dreamy expression on his face. He looks like a child thinking as it plays. At this moment, it would look entirely natural if he were holding a ball, a toy train or a horse on wheels.

'Paolo, what's wrong?'

And she bends to put the bags down.

He turns his head towards her like the periscope of a submarine.

'Would you give me some water, please?'

'Oh my God, Paolo, what's happened, did you fall?' She hurries to her husband, only now beginning to suspect that the situation might be more serious than she thought.

He doesn't reply as she touches him, strokes him, searches his hair for a wound, a bruise, anything.

'You're OK, you're OK,' she says, talking more to herself than to him. 'You didn't fall, did you? How do you feel, what happened?'

And when she tries to pull him to his feet, she encounters an obstinate, painful resistance, as though he is attached to the floor by his clothes.

She looks at him, terrified. Her husband's face is frozen in the sweet and impotent expression of someone ashamed of being ill, but who has no wish to be helped back to a painful state of lucidity.

She gets to her feet, her hand over her mouth. Then she calls the ambulance and, immediately after that, Celeste.

But at that moment Celeste is posting a letter in a busy street, and she doesn't hear her mobile ringing in the outer pocket of her backpack.

'So did you buy the dress or not?' Heller asks Varika, having found her easily, simply by walking along the coast.

When he saw her she was quite a long way from the restaurant where he had first met her, and she was walking along the edge of the road, looking out to sea and dragging an old umbrella behind her. Heller parked under the straw awnings opposite, and felt a heady rush of admiration at seeing her so exposed, so completely alone and immune to the fear of the traffic. Then, without moving from his car, he hooted his horn at her and she came over to him, with the sea behind her and her long hair whipping against her face, surprised and happy that he'd come back.

'I haven't got all the money yet,' the girl replies, intrigued by the little secret she shares with him.

'Don't forget you promised to let me see it,' says Heller.

Varika hides her face, playing with the remains of the umbrella that she has found on the ground. In the other hand she holds a wooden disc with the key rings hanging from it.

'I've got something to show you, too,' says Heller. And from the back seat he raises a small cage, holding it level with Varika's eyes. The girl squeals with excitement. From behind the thin bars a Siamese kitten, with deliciously squinting eyes and a hook-shaped tail, tries to touch her with its little paws, making tiny high-pitched mewing sounds.

Giggling with delight, Varika jumps up and down on the spot and asks if she can hold the animal. Heller takes the kitten from the cage and hands it to her, reminding her to be gentle.

Clawing at the girl's sweatshirt, the kitten clings to it and tries stubbornly to climb up it, seemingly hoping to reach her face and climb that as well. Almost embarrassed by such an explicit demonstration of intent, Varika brings the kitten back down to her belly and strokes it, laughing excitedly as it purrs.

Heller takes the animal from her hands and puts it back in the cage.

'We've got to go now,' he says with a hint of regret.

'Stay a little while,' she says.

'No, it's late. The kitten needs feeding and I haven't made up its basket for the night. It was only given to me a little while ago,' Heller explains, and acts as though he is about to turn on the engine, slowly and carefully measuring out each gesture.

'Will you bring it when you come back?' she asks.

Heller makes a massive effort to suppress the terrible frisson of elation that he feels as the girl falls into the trap.

'Oh, I don't know, it's so small. And it's a cat, cats like to stay at home, not like dogs, which you can take for a walk,' he replies. Only then does he turn the key in the ignition.

'Can I come to your house?' the girl asks, right on time, overcoming her embarrassment and her fear that he might leave before she gets the opportunity to ask him.

'Of course, why not?' he replies distractedly, starting to drive away. 'Next time I'll fetch you, so that you can come and play with the kitten.'

And as he waves goodbye and pulls out into the road,

he looks at her eyes, already full of expectation. As he drives off, he feels so excited that he would sound his horn like a lunatic, if he could.

19

Among the prisoners being escorted by the guards who crowd into the judge's antechamber for the preliminary hearings, a young man of about twenty-five, tall, with handcuffs around his wrists, awaits his turn, weeping steadily. The policeman accompanying him tries to console him, talking to him in a low voice as the prisoner repeats that he hasn't had anything to eat for two days.

Finally the office door opens, and the clerk of the court, a bald little man with a moustache, calls out the name of the young man, who wipes his face with his forearm. The policeman's hand, behind the young man's back, guides him towards the office.

At that moment Heller arrives, running and very elegantly dressed.

'Here I am,' he says, turning towards the clerk, who is still standing in the office doorway holding a bundle of papers.

'Ah, good morning, Mr Heller, my apologies if our phone call disturbed you.'

'That's fine,' says Heller, 'I was virtually here anyway.'

The young man frowns at him with the slightly haughty diffidence usually reserved for duty lawyers, who tend to be treated, initially at least, as intruders, exploiters of other people's desperation.

It is like a mother tongue to Heller, that look, that ostentatious lack of respect for the person playing this role that wasn't requested but is nonetheless required by law, hence suspect and therefore despised. And although he understands this attitude and even, to an extent, approves of it, he reacts with an equal and opposite aloofness, taking refuge in the detachment from the other man's tragedy that is an essential aspect of his profession.

Then he enters the judge's office behind the hand-cuffed wretch as unaffectedly as a plumber arriving to replace a washer; he listens carefully to the arraignment for the crime (aggravated robbery, of which he is accused along with a number of co-defendants who have already been questioned); he memorises the circumstances of the arrest and the evidence that is in the prosecution's possession; he closes his eyes as the young man stupidly denies the accusation, blaming his accomplices; he predicts the reaction of the magistrate who, precisely on cue, shows the young man the record of the confiscated stolen goods found in his cellar after his arrest (a moped, a digital camera, a laptop and a car radio); he requests that the magistrate pretend not to have heard the young man threaten self-harm should he be returned to jail; then, following a script of unspoken exchanges with the judge, he begins to guide his client's replies, manoeuvring them in the least damaging legal direction: he has him say that he kept the goods with a view to buying only some of them, thus making him confess to an attempt to receive stolen goods, to balance the blunt denial of his participation in the theft (which has in any case been confirmed by the declarations of his accomplices), thus leading to a request for house arrest that the magistrate proves entirely willing to grant.

Meanwhile, he thinks about all the other occasions on which he has heard the same words issuing from his mouth in precisely the same order, and how predictable and endlessly repeatable is the protocol of normality that he acts out every day. There's no point to any of it. Nothing is resolved. My function is purely formulaic. I don't give a damn about this boy and his stupid crimes. His pitiful haul depresses me. His future is a matter of utter indifference to me. His rights are bits of photo-copied paper. No one here believes in what he is doing. The handcuffed criminal is lying, the guard escorting him is lying, the lawyer is lying, the judge is lying. The clerks, the typists and the office staff are lying. The Bar Council is lying, the Criminal Court is lying, the forensic scientists and their journals are lying. The meetings, the assemblies and the TV channels are lying. The journalists and their interviewees are lying.

I'm just one lie among the rest.

The confirmatory hearing concludes with the granting of house arrest. The young man beams, and immediately asks the guard to remove his handcuffs. At the door, he steels himself to approach Heller.

'I wanted to thank you,' he says hesitantly.

'You should have done that when I arrived,' Heller replies.

The boy lowers his head.

'Just make sure you don't leave your house, or you'll end up back inside,' Heller adds. And the young man nods as he walks away.

Half an hour later Heller is back at his building. He leaves his car outside the garage, sounding the horn twice so that the valets will come and park it. He greets the porter, who is snoozing in his lodge, and as he walks to the lift he sees from a distance an envelope poking out from the slit of his mailbox.

Strange. He picked up his mail before leaving that morning.

'Did the postman come again, or something?' he loudly asks the porter as he turns back on himself and slips his key into the box.

'No,' the porter replies, still half dazed from sleep as he emerges from his office, as if belatedly demonstrating his efficiency.

'Then what's that letter doing in there?' asks Heller, losing his temper.

The porter looks at him feebly.

Heller removes the envelope. There's nothing written on it, on either side. A shiver runs down his spine as though under the pressure of an outspread palm.

'Can you tell me what you're up to if anyone can get in here and leave whatever he feels like, without your noticing?'

It's the first time in thirteen years that he has raised his voice to the porter, who gulps in humiliation.

'You may as well go back to sleep,' Heller breaks off, heading for the stairs and tearing open one side of the envelope.

He opens it by the lift. And when he sees what's inside he starts to sweat. He doesn't know exactly what he is feeling, but he thinks it is pain. Growing, retroactive pain.

Three polaroids, each with a date printed on it, in sequence.

The first shows only the face. Slightly out of focus, because the camera is so close. The girl's head rests delicately on a bed of damp leaves. You can still see the pallor where the adhesive tape has been pulled from her lips. They wear a kind of smile, which he doesn't remember.

In the second, the torso. The name. Slightly faded, but perfectly legible. The skin around the nipples has assumed the colour of a bruise, as though the child had been struck by two blows delivered simultaneously to her chest.

In the third, the feet. Sweet, dirty, pale. The nails blackened by death.

Heller loosens his tie, glancing round as if there is something he needs to do, and then he stands where he is, frozen by an inchoate sense of urgency that impels him, but doesn't tell him where. He hides the photographs in the envelope and supports himself with one hand against the outer door of the lift, which is just about to arrive. He turns the handle that opens the door, without actually getting in. He is distraught, but lucid enough to acknowledge that he has no right to suffer for this betrayal of his trust.

Someone on one of the upper floors strikes repeatedly against the column of the shaft, summoning the lift. An arrogant, offensive sound that unleashes in Heller a hunger for violence. He throws the lift door open to keep it from moving. Then he climbs the stairs three at a time.

On the third floor he finds the waiting man. He's a tenant, a recent arrival, Heller must have met him a couple of times, but he doesn't even know what the man's name is. He is big and doughy, in his forties. In one hand he holds a battered shoulder bag.

'What are you banging for, eh? What's the big hurry?' Heller says to him, advancing on him, excited by his rage.

The man adjusts his glasses on his nose.

'Sorry, I didn't know . . .' he says awkwardly.

'Really? And what didn't you know? That someone would come up here and smash your face in?' says Heller, grabbing him by the shirt, in the middle of his chest.

The man drops his bag and grips Heller's arm with both hands. He already has flecks of spittle at the corners of his mouth. Heller holds him with one hand and contracts his muscles as he lifts the man into the air. He is still holding his briefcase in the other hand.

The man pants, his eyes wide with disbelief. He tries to cling onto Heller's arm as though it were his only way of defending himself.

At that moment Heller is overwhelmed with self-contempt. And he immediately turns it on his victim.

'Do that again,' he whispers, 'and I'll smack you into that wall.'

Then he leaves him. The man licks his lips, picks his bag off the floor and struggles painfully to regain his composure.

As he descends the stairs, Heller experiences a sensation of nausea at the thought that from now on the wretched man will treat him with much greater respect than he did before.

He goes out into the street, passing in front of the porter's lodge. This time the porter is careful not to come out.

Heller's car is still parked by the garage entrance. He walks over to it, opens the door and gets in, throwing his briefcase onto the passenger seat, and drives off.

Within fifteen minutes he's at the coast. She isn't there. OK, he thinks. And he purses his lips, making a promise to himself. Then he starts driving around in circles. With each fruitless turning he takes he feels his rage mounting, and it gives him a sharp sense of pleasure. Seeing Heller pass again and again, a man selling contraband cigarettes eventually waves at him.

Celeste comes by bus. As always, she gets off two stops early so as to walk the rest of the way. Heller, who is just heading back, recognises her immediately, twenty metres ahead of him. At first he stares at her with awe, finding her face mysterious and significant. Then, for fear of losing hold of the fury he has been cultivating until that moment, he stamps his foot down on the accelerator and catches up with her.

Celeste starts at the screech of brakes. Instinctively, she raises an arm to protect herself. Heller is wounded by the gesture, but he maintains his concentration. He gets out of the car and walks towards her, stiffly, like an automaton. The heads of the people at the bus stop crane round. A car slows but then continues on its way. Celeste shields herself with her arm again when Heller catches up. He grips her wrists with both hands.

'What do you want from me? Tell me! Do you want to report me? Is that it? Harass me? What is it?' he says, clutching her harder and harder.

Celeste bites her lip in pain.

'Let go of my hands. Let go, please.'

More distraught than angry, Heller pushes her away before immediately grabbing her again, clutching her by the neck with his left hand, as though overcome by an irrepressible desire to self-destruct. Celeste kicks out at his shins. Aroused by the pain, Heller snarls and tightens his grip. Somebody starts walking slowly towards them from the bus stop. Celeste, her eyes full of tears, tries to pull away from him, wheezing faintly. Three people, one of them a woman, have joined them.

'Leave her alone, you bastard,' says the woman.

For Heller this is like a bucket of cold water. He suddenly relaxes his grip, seized by a feeling of compassion that almost overwhelms him. He remains motionless, his arm still outstretched, as Celeste throws herself to one side, coughing convulsively. Two cars stop, but no one gets out.

Horrified, Heller looks at Celeste, who is now crouching on the footpath, overbalanced by her backpack, gasping for air, clutching her belly. He bends helplessly over her, and slowly lays a twitching hand on her shoulder.

'Get me a drink, please, some water,' she says.

Heller gets back to his feet and looks round, passing his gaze over the contemptuous and still frightened faces of the few people who have summoned the courage to get involved. He sees a café on the other side of the road, and runs over to it. He returns almost immediately with a plastic cup. Celeste is still sitting on the pavement. The woman is beside her, gently speaking to her. Of the others, one is walking uncertainly back to the bus stop, while the other is keying a number into his mobile phone. Heller bends over Celeste, ignoring the contempt of the woman, who stands motionless behind him. He hands Celeste the cup of water. He hears the woman cursing him in a low voice, but he's not bothered by her.

Celeste drinks greedily, then takes a deep breath with her mouth wide open. Slowly, Heller straightens up. The woman stares at him bravely. Then he turns on his heel and goes back to his car.

As he switches the engine on, he notices the man on the opposite pavement, his arms folded, his head to one side. The man looks at him slyly and smiles.

20

Over the next few days, Heller doesn't leave home, even
to go to court. When the phone rings, he checks the
caller's number or lets the answering machine take it so
that he can decide whether or not to take the call. And
he never does. He misses out on a complex case without
giving any excuse, aware that he risks being had for
contempt.

By now the kitten has taken possession of the flat. It
slips into every nook and cranny, pounces on the smallest
objects, sleeps on top of the television. The only room
from which it is excluded is the kitchen, because of the
budgerigar.

Heller spends his time waiting for something to
happen. He doesn't touch a single case file, he eats hardly
anything, he just sleeps. His sole occupation consists of
carrying the chocolate eggs he bought a few days
previously around the flat, and distributing them,
according to some crazed logic, along a trail that starts at
the front door and ends up in the bedroom.

When he hears the entryphone early one afternoon,
he is busy changing the cat's litter.

'Mr Heller, it's Bambacaro here. Could you come
down, please?'

One of the policemen from the court, a man he has met many times, at various questionings and other judicial occasions. He has always got on particularly well with him.

'Bambacaro, hi. What's up?'

'Please come down, Mr Heller.'

The request is made very slowly, clearly revealing the policeman to be reluctantly following orders.

'Fine, just a minute,' Heller replies. And without even changing his clothes he takes his jacket from the coat-rack, checks that he has his keys, and leaves the flat.

The policeman, in plain clothes, is aimlessly pacing the courtyard of the building, his hands in his pockets, as he waits for Heller.

'Here I am,' says the latter as he arrives, 'is something up?'

'Hello, Avvocato. No, nothing. You're just to come to the court with me for a moment.'

'To the court, now? Why?'

'Dr Vignarelli wants to see you.'

Heller starts at the name. He remembers, as though in a photograph, the bitter expression stamped on the magistrate's face on the day of the exams.

'Vignarelli? Why?' he asks.

'That I can't tell you,' replies the policeman.

Heller realises he has asked a stupid question.

'And he couldn't call me, so you had to go to all this trouble?'

'Mr Heller, please don't ask me what I don't know.'

What I don't know. Sounded like: What I can't tell you.

'Fine, let's go,' Heller blurts out, driven by a desire to get it over with. 'My car's in the garage opposite.'

The policeman holds him back with a hand.

'No, don't worry. We'll go in ours,' he says, as though observing protocol as a statutory escort.

Heller could easily question the propriety of the task to which the policeman has been assigned, but his sympathy for him, and his perverse desire to know what is going on, persuade him to play along.

During the journey the policeman talks about other things. Heller replies, discovering that he is relieved at the idea that he might finally be about to find himself in a predictable situation.

At this hour of the afternoon, the court is practically empty. Only the public prosecutor's offices are open, and not even all of those. Heller and the policeman stop at Vignarelli's door. Bambacaro knocks lightly, then opens the door, just enough to frame in the doorway the figure of the magistrate sitting at his desk.

'Dr Vignarelli, Avvocato Heller is here.'

'Thanks, Bambacaro. Show him in.'

The policeman steps aside for Heller, who thanks him with a nod of the head. Then the officer closes the door again, leaving the lawyer alone with the magistrate.

Before saying anything, Vignarelli puts on the reading glasses that hang on a string around his collar, picks up a file from a pile of papers lined up to his left and opens it. Heller remains where he is, motionless and silent, waiting.

'Sit down, Heller,' says the magistrate, indicating the armchair on the far side of the desk with a wave of his hand.

I would prefer not to, thinks Heller, trying not to smile. Then he sits down, weaving his fingers around his right knee as he crosses his legs.

'Are you acquainted with a girl by the name of Celeste Calitri?' Vignarelli asks, consulting his papers.

Heller replies as though doing him a favour.

'If the surname of the girl I have in mind is indeed Calitri, then yes, I do know her.'

'What is your relationship with her?'

Heller folds his arms, raising his eyes towards the ceiling and then slowly back down to rest on the magistrate.

'Will you tell me what you're up to, Dr Vignarelli, and by what right you have summoned me? Am I under investigation? Because if I am, I think we've jumped a few steps.'

Vignarelli is extremely serious.

'Had I wished to take formal action, Avvocato Heller, I would have done so already. This is an entirely private and informal conversation. You are free to leave if you wish to do so.'

'I know precisely what I can do, Dr Vignarelli. I also know perfectly well what you can't do.'

'Fine,' the magistrate replies, ignoring the provocation, 'so are you staying or going?'

For once Heller is stumped for a reply.

Vignarelli shuts the file and opens it again.

'I have here a statement bringing an accusation against you, signed by the girl's mother, Altomira Calitri. Do you know her, too?'

Heller clicks his tongue.

'The name doesn't mean much to me, but yes, I think I know who we're talking about.'

Vignarelli folds his arms and rests them on the file.

'Will you please tell me the nature of your relationship with the girl?'

It is probably the repetition of the question that prompts Heller's sarcastic reply.

'Look, Dr Vignarelli, if you want to question me this isn't the appropriate procedure. Do you want me to explain how it's done?'

Vignarelli slams his open hand against the desk. His pen-holders nearly topple over.

'Enough of this nonsense, Heller! With all the evidence against you, you might consider wiping that smirk off your face! I'm doing you a big favour here, I don't know if you realise that, but if you try to offend me once more I shall let you know in no uncertain terms whether or not I am familiar with legal process!'

Heller falls silent, caught off guard by the man's anger. He has the same flushed face, the same trembling lips, the same wounded dignity as he had that time at the exams.

'I don't like you, as you know very well,' Vignarelli resumes, beginning to moderate his tone, 'but I have sufficient respect for you as a lawyer to consider it my duty to call you in privately to discuss the serious allegations being made against you before proceeding down the official route. And I am not, as you might imagine, so callous as to take advantage of the situation and drag it into an inquiry that could ruin your career before first hearing your version of events.'

This unexpected explanation, at once furious and sincere, sweeps away the procedural irregularity to which until that moment Heller thought he was being subjected, and fills him with a sudden admiration for the magistrate. He looks at the man, mortified by his rectitude, as he struggles to find the words to tell him how sorry he is.

'I'm sorry, Dr Vignarelli. I beg your forgiveness with all my heart. But don't waste your time on me. All the accusations made against me are true.'

'What's true?'

'Everything written in that complaint.'

'I haven't even told you what it says.'

'I can imagine.'

'Pleading guilty to an accusation without first knowing what it is. I'm startled to hear such an idea from the mouth of a lawyer of your experience.'

Heller thinks he is blushing. He wants to say to the magistrate: I no longer give a damn about my profession, my status, myself, or any accusation that anyone in the world might throw at me. Please proceed, and let's get it over with. And he probably would, had Vignarelli not suddenly grown so much in his estimation.

'So,' the magistrate insists, 'you admit you know this underage girl, you admit that you have had a relationship with her, you admit that you have attacked her, raped and beaten her.'

Brutally raped and beaten her? Heller feels his jaw drop, as these last words fall unwilled from his lips.

'Are those the accusations the mother makes in her complaint?' he asks.

'Not the mother, Heller. The girl. Those are her exact words as recorded upon her admission to hospital, written in her medical report and confirmed in a statement delivered a few hours later.'

Heller opens his eyes wide. A gratuitous and incomprehensible stab in the back. A pain which, if he believed in the clichés of emotions, he would have located at the exact centre of his heart.

'A number of witnesses attest that they saw you attacking the girl in the middle of the street.'

'That is true,' Heller admits, looking at the floor.

I believe you, Vignarelli's silence seems to say.

'According to these witnesses, you turned up, at the wheel of your car, braked abruptly by the girl and got out of the car, hurling yourself furiously at her. There was a scuffle and you tried to strangle her.'

'It's true.'

'You then became concerned about her and brought her a glass of water that you went to fetch from a nearby café.'

'It's all true.'

'And then?'

'Then what?'

'You attacked the girl in the street, and then what did

you do? You're not going to try and tell me you raped and beat her on the spot.'

Raped. Beat.

As he drove away, Heller had seen that bastard on the opposite footpath.

You've been clever, he thinks.

Fine, so that was what you wanted.

'Why are you smiling, Heller?'

'No reason. Ignore my reactions, Dr Vignarelli. I have no intention of causing you any problems. I admit all the accusations.'

Vignarelli stares at him for a moment before speaking again.

'Who are you covering for, Heller?'

'Who am I what?'

'You understood me very well. Come on, tell me.'

'I have nothing to tell, Dr Vignarelli. The report is true.'

Vignarelli glances around the room, and then starts again.

'I know how poorly you think of me, Avvocato. But I have been a magistrate long enough to recognise an innocent man.'

'No, you're wrong. I'm guilty. Very guilty.'

Vignarelli exhales.

'Fine, then tell me what you did to the girl.'

'All the things you're accusing me of.'

'Are you joking? I want you to tell me exactly what you did to her, where, in what order and in what way.'

'I beat her and raped her.'

'You haven't answered my question.'

'You're asking me to remember very unpleasant details.'

'Don't try to evade the question, Heller. Come on, answer me.'

'My memory isn't being much help to me at the moment.'

'Fine, then tell me whether or not you were armed. You'll remember that, at least.'

'I could have been.'

'You could have been?'

'I was furious, I don't remember.'

'Do you really expect me to believe you?'

'That's neither here nor there. I intend to assume responsibility for the crimes ascribed to me. I attacked the girl in the presence of many witnesses, she has made a statement against me, I am prepared to admit my guilt. That should be enough for you to take the appropriate measures.'

'Do you want to ruin your career? Destroy your life? Is that what you're trying to do?'

Heller doesn't reply.

'I have never liked you, Heller, but I don't think you're guilty. I'm less and less convinced of it.'

'That's very noble of you, Dr Vignarelli. And for what it's worth, I feel mortified about the way I treated you that time at the exams, and today as well.'

'I refuse to be your accomplice, Heller. Your masochistic tendencies mean nothing to me. We haven't seen each other, this meeting has been entirely informal.

And I count on you to respect this privacy agreement between us. At the moment I will not request that you be taken into custody, because I don't think you're guilty. I will officially examine the report, which was only presented a few days ago. In the meantime I will investigate this girl, the life she leads, the truth about the relationship you had with her. Then I will establish what needs to be done.'

'You can't, Dr Vignarelli. If I acknowledge my guilt, confirming the accusations made against me, it is your duty to proceed on the basis of the evidence at your disposal.'

'Stop there, Heller. I'm offering you an opportunity. Think about it. Go home. And call me when you've come sufficiently to your senses to tell me the truth.'

Heller gets up from his chair, looking with helpless admiration at the magistrate, who pretends to immerse himself in another case file, and walks towards the door.

'Heller.'

Heller turns around.

'I won't wait for more than a few days.'

Heller leaves the magistrate's office and closes the door. At the end of the corridor he sees Bambacaro, who is smoking as he waits. He walks towards him.

'Do you want me to drive you back?' the policeman asks as Heller comes up to him.

'No, Bambacaro, thank you. I'd rather go on foot,' he replies. And he stands there in a daze, watching the officer blow smoke from his mouth.

When you've made your mind up, send a smoke

signal. Just say my name. Whatever you need.

'Everything all right, Avvocato?' Bambacaro asks, slightly alarmed.

'Fine,' Heller replies, with a sudden gleam in his eyes. And he walks down the stairs, repeating in his mind the digits of the number that he has memorised like a date of birth.

In the street he makes a call from a phone box not far from the Palace of Justice.

21

Over the weekend Heller cuddles the cat, continues minutely adjusting the position of the little baskets of chocolate eggs around his flat, and uses up an entire cartridge of ink signing letters giving up each of his cases, discovering that nothing has ever made him feel more serene than throwing away a whole life's work.

Every now and again, after signing each letter at the bottom, he looks around him.

The books, the furniture, the walls. The city outside the window. He will lose everything, once and for all.

It doesn't seem like much of a problem.

On Monday afternoon, returning from the supermarket with shopping for himself and the cat, he finds the lift occupied. He waits for a moment; then, seeing that the red light is showing no sign of going out, he gives up. The cat litter is heavy as he climbs the stairs.

At the foot of the last flight that leads to his floor, he sees Celeste by the door. From such a short distance he can clearly make out the swelling on her upper lip and a yellowish bruise running from the bottom of her right eye to halfway down her cheek. For some reason he doesn't particularly react when he sees her.

'Why have you come?' he asks her as he climbs the last step, a little breathlessly, because of the weight he is carrying.

She shrugs. Then she offers to relieve him of one of the bags.

Heller lets her do it, takes out his keys and opens the door. Celeste comes in immediately behind him. She follows him to the kitchen, noticing that the door is shut. Heller turns the handle, looking at the floor. He moves carefully, sideways, so as to open the door as little as possible.

'Shut it,' he says.

Celeste is about to do so when something darts between her feet, slipping through the half-open door.

'I told you to shut it,' says Heller, putting the shopping down on the table. Then he runs off to recover the kitten, which is already circling at the foot of the budgie's cage seeking a way of climbing up. Celeste thinks of Tweety and Sylvester. Heller lifts the kitten between pinched fingers, bunching the fur at its shoulder blades. The kitten looks around with its squinting little eyes, wondering what it's suddenly doing in mid-air. Heller sets it back down outside the kitchen and closes the door. The cat immediately starts scratching at the glass door, mewing piteously in the hope of moving him to relent. After a while it realises that this is a waste of time, and wanders off, still protesting.

'I didn't know you had a cat,' says Celeste.

'I didn't until a few days ago,' says Heller. He opens the

fridge door and takes a jar of mayonnaise, a net of oranges, a double pack of yoghurt and half a litre of milk out of the shopping bag. Then he starts putting them away.

'Has it got a name?'

'No. Or rather yes, sometimes I call it Scratch.'

'Scratch. I like that, it's original.'

'No, it isn't. It was in an old film.'

'Oh. Siamese, isn't it?'

'Mm.'

'It's gorgeous.'

'Yep.'

'A present?'

'Not really.'

'How old is it?'

'About a month and a half.'

'Why are you nervous?'

'I'm not nervous.'

'Yeah, right.'

'I said I'm not.'

'Of course you are. You're getting irritable talking about the cat.'

'I'm not getting irritable, why should I be?'

'You don't want to talk about it.'

Heller slams the oranges down on the middle shelf of the fridge. The shelf slips off its rails and hangs at an angle onto the one below. A jar of anchovies remains upright, against the odds.

'OK, fine! You're right, I don't want to! Just change the subject, OK?'

Celeste looks at Heller as though trying to translate him. He carries on putting things away, turning his back on her.

'Can I pick it up?' Celeste asks after a while.

'As long as you don't let it back in here,' says Heller without turning round, still irritable, but speaking more quietly now.

Celeste carefully opens the door, steps out of the kitchen and shuts the door again. She is immediately drawn by a pile of metallic red chocolates gleaming from a little basket resting on the hall radiator.

Heller finishes putting the shopping away, then goes to find her. She is in the sitting room, on the sofa. The kitten has mistaken her sweatshirt for its mother's breasts, judging by the way it is climbing pathetically up to her, stretching and relaxing its claws, plunging its muzzle into the fabric in search of non-existent nipples.

Heller stands frozen between the corridor and the door, feeling the awkward itch of someone who wants to talk and can't.

He goes to the window, opens the curtains, looks into the street with great interest, and closes them again. He puts his hand in his pockets. He lets his eyes wander around the room as though someone has moved the furniture around without his knowing.

'Why did you report me?' he asks finally.

He faces away from her as he puts the question.

Waiting for him to turn round, Celeste strokes the cat, one hand following the other.

'Because it was what you wanted,' she replies.

A void, an abyss. The stream flowing suddenly away. Like dropping into a hole that has suddenly opened up in the floor. Heller feels himself plunging, his voice won't come, the light is high up, far away, further and further up, he waits for the bottom, the crash, he flails his arms and legs, nothing to hold onto.

He looks at her. He looks into those simple eyes that refuse to judge him. He doesn't even know what colour they are. Once again he wonders why this little girl has come out of nowhere to fill a place in his life, and how it is that she conveys to him an indefinable passivity which suggests that no reply would be of any particular significance. Once again he feels exposed and thus truly understood. The gratitude that suddenly fills him, turning him towards Celeste as a child turns to its mother, stifles any fear, any temptation to aggression, any violence. He is very ashamed, now, to have been hostile towards her just a short time ago, in the kitchen. He despises himself for still having said nothing about the bruises on her face. He walks over to her and crouches down. He raises his right hand, opens it, and moves it towards her like a blind man trying to recognise someone dear to him. The cat purrs noisily. Celeste pulls away, then lets him touch her. Heller brushes the outline of her face with the tip of his index finger.

'It was that guy, wasn't it?'

'Yes,' she replies with a sigh.

'He won't hurt you again,' says Heller.

Celeste glances at him, suddenly frightened. Heller gets up, regretting having said what he has just said. He faces the window again, turning his back on her. The next time he looks around, Celeste is gone. But the cat is curled up and asleep. Heller moves to the middle of the room, looking in all directions. He sees her. She is in the bedroom, by the chest of drawers. She's looking at something. He joins her, afraid that she might have worked it all out.

He leans against the door frame. Celeste turns gently, picking a chocolate egg from another basket on the chest of drawers.

'Will you let me have one of these, too?'

Heller is embarrassed.

Celeste unwraps the chocolate and puts it in her mouth. She sucks it. Tastes it. Chews it. Swallows it.

'You want to do it again, don't you?'

Heller thinks he's blushing.

'What did you say?'

Celeste ignores his pointless question.

'In this room, is that it?'

'What are you saying, Celeste?'

She stiffens, surprised. It's the first time he has called her by her name. She starts talking again, as though she doesn't require his answers.

'The cat was the giveaway.'

Heller shifts his gaze away from hers. He is convinced that, whatever he says, his voice would tremble.

Celeste comes over to him.

'Tell me.'

Heller goes on hiding. He is in the corner, no longer willing to lie to her, wanting to reach rock bottom.

He nods, with difficulty.

Celeste goes and sits on the bed. When she opens her mouth again, it is as though she is speaking with a different voice.

'I want to watch.'

Heller freezes in the doorway. This time he doesn't pretend not to have understood.

He stares at her with astonishment.

And an obscene kind of delight.

22

The car stinks of cigarettes stubbed out long ago. The man looks at the darkness on the other side of the window. He thinks about his dog, and he is upset.

Someone's looking for you, they'd told him. But he hadn't believed it. When they left he tried to ask. They didn't reply. They aren't talking to him, they aren't talking to each other. As though they can't stand each other. Or don't know each other.

The one who's driving is the oldest. He must be at least fifty, and he's wearing a tie. The other two have a similar build, squat and stocky, and the same fixed stare.

The man is sitting in the back seat, with his jailer beside him, transported but without constraint, free to move, to behave like any ordinary passenger. An imposition of normality that leaves him more enslaved and humiliated than a gun to the temple.

They haven't gone all that far. They're still on the coast road. The place he knows best, his territory.

The car turns onto a little path that runs through a copse of pine trees before veering off towards the sea. After a while they stop in front of a small two-storey house surrounded by fairly high walls.

The first to get out is the man sitting next to the

driver. Like a chauffeur manoeuvre, he walks around the car to the back door and opens it. He looks as if he's thinking about something else, a deliberately distracted air, designed to intimidate.

The man stares at his neighbour.

Realising the impracticability of any attempt at escape or struggle, he looks at each of his kidnappers in turn and gets out of the car.

They push him into the garden of the villa and shut the gate behind him.

The door and the windows of the house are closed. No one waiting for him. The garden is bare, a few untended plants, not even any garden furniture. From the other side of the gate, the three men watch him in silence.

As if he has felt them a thousand times before, he recognises the symptoms of deadly terror. He starts to move nervously along the boundary wall in search of a foothold that might enable him to climb it, however pointless such an initiative might seem given the presence of his jailers outside. He tries to jump up, but his hands fail to hook over the top of the wall and he keeps falling back down. Then he walks back to take a run-up, and tries to leap higher. Then he hears a faint sound, the sense of something huge suddenly filling the air, before an enormous weight lands on his back, and tremendously powerful jaws sink their teeth into his right shoulder.

Dogs he knows about. Even in the twilight that obscures the outlines of things to reveal only the centre of the close-up image, he recognises the unmistakeable features of a Rottweiler. Male, judging by its size. Its neck broad and nervous. Almond-shaped eyes, so sweet. Slender, perhaps even a bit bony in its build. From the way it is studying him in search of the nearest and most vulnerable point to bite into, he concludes that it has been properly trained. He knows how strong and stubborn these dogs are when it comes to fighting. And even in the anxiety of the moment he can appreciate the perfection of the dog's bared teeth.

Blood spills copiously from the ugly wound that the animal has opened in his flesh, just above the collarbone. The man tries to ignore the pain, and prepare himself for the next assault. Crouching low, he clenches his fists and protects his face with his forearms pressed tightly together. The pugilist's defensive posture. He waits for the dog to leap, then swiftly turns around and rolls himself into a ball with his head between his knees, presenting his back to the dog. He hears its jaws snapping at the air behind him, unable to find the necessary purchase. He endures the ferocious onslaught of claws scratching at him in a bid to make him turn around, lacerating his shirt, his skin, his flesh. He grits his teeth with pain as he shields his terrified body from the enemy on top of him.

After a few attempts the dog stops, yelping with frustration. Then it starts circling him, in search of a breach in his defences. The man looks at the creature through the gap between his arms. Its teeth are bloodstained, horrifying, demoniacal, its eyes filled with a stubborn desire to fulfil its function as a guard dog.

The man leans his head to cover the wound on his shoulder, which is still bleeding, sapping his strength. Convulsive tremors run down his spine. Snarling, the Rottweiler jumps, landing on him with all its power and knocking him over. The man hugs himself with his arms with all the strength he can muster. The dog grabs him by one calf. Before it has time to tighten its jaws, the man kicks it hard, freeing himself, springs backwards, makes a bayonet of his right hand, clenches the muscles of his fingers to the point of spasm, and strikes the dog violently in the eye.

Blinded, the Rottweiler recoils, resting on its back feet, rocking back and forth and yelping. Then it begins to wander dazedly around, stamping its feet at random, waiting for its eyesight to return. The man immediately takes advantage of this distraction to escape to the gate. Gripping the bars, he launches himself upwards. He doesn't even have time to get off the ground before a violent blow, delivered with an object that feels as if it might be made of iron, ruthlessly crushes his fingers against the bars, loosening his grip. As he falls backwards, he sees on the other side of the gate one of his jailers holding the gun with which he has just struck him. His hand is still in mid-air, in a chopping position.

The man hears the snarl of the dog returning to its task. He turns round, terrified, weakened, as though seeing the creature for the first time. He has run out of time. The animal grabs him by the back of his left leg, a few inches above his knee. This time the guard dog has got a good grip, and won't let go. He lets out a visceral, penetrating scream. He clenches his fists and starts desperately striking the animal about the head, but the Rottweiler goes on tightening its jaws until it finally brings down its prey, dragging him far from the gate. There it worries at its victim until he abandons the desire to defend himself, before finally tearing his throat out. The screams become whimpers, and the dog's snarl settles into the methodical rhythm of its working jaws.

By the time the three men enter the garden, the man is drenched in blood. He's still fighting, but more and more weakly. The Rottweiler crouches a short distance away from him, in a mournful position of repose. It looks vacantly at the newcomers, then rises up on its back feet, preparing to attack once more. The oldest of the three is holding a torch in one hand and the pistol in the other. He switches on the torch, aims it straight at the dog's head and fires along the trajectory of the beam.

The projectile strikes the animal between the right eye and ear. The Rottweiler stands stock-still for a moment before it attempts to move and then topples heavily on one side. The man fires again, twice: one bullet sticks in the shutter of a ground-floor window, another in one of the two steps in front of the door. Then he clicks the trigger to check that the weapon is empty. He rubs the butt of the pistol on a flap of his jacket, and then steps towards the man on the ground. The other two remain by the gate, motionless as sentries.

*

The following afternoon, policemen from the local station find the corpse in a corner of the garden, not far from the carcass of the Rottweiler. The weapon found in the victim's hand clearly suggests that the man (a previous offender already known to the policemen who find his body) entered the garden of the villa with the aim of burgling it and, having been surprised by the guard dog, drew his pistol too late to defend himself, firing at random before finally hitting the animal, which had by then repeatedly savaged him, leading to his death from loss of blood.

The public prosecutor has only to read through the police statement to be in no doubt as to the sequence of events. He even considers the possibility of taking action against the owner of the villa. However, the presence of a dog in the garden had been properly indicated by a sign to that effect, which was clearly visible from outside the property. A quick telephone call to the appropriate office reveals that the relevant tax had been kept regularly up to date.

23

Celeste, with the kitten snoozing in her arms, waits in the corridor. The house seems to breathe. Everything's ready.

When she hears the lift stop at her floor, she takes the cat into the study and shuts the door. Then she heads towards the bedroom.

Heller and Varika enter immediately afterwards. Celeste can make out their voices perfectly. The child is asking about the kitten. And Heller, as planned, brings her into the study.

Celeste opens the wardrobe. She pushes aside the few clothes hanging there, and climbs in.

The kitten is curled up on the armchair beside the window. The curtain is closed. Varika runs towards the kitten, which raises its head. She jumps up and down on the spot, repeating a word in her own language, something that sounds to Heller like a proper name. The little animal starts purring even before she picks it up.

Heller asks her if she wants a Coke.

'Yes,' she says, as she presses the kitten to her neck.

Celeste crouches in the wardrobe and pulls the door towards her, leaving it open a crack. Two lines of dialogue reach her clearly.

'Is this your office?'

'Yes.'

Then her thoughts are lost in darkness. It's quite nice, being in a wardrobe.

She has almost fallen asleep when a guttural laugh from the girl makes her start. The echo is amplified inside the wardrobe as she waits again, concentrating on the voices that reach her, muffled now. She thinks they are talking about chocolate and eggs.

'There are more if you can find them,' he is saying.

Celeste readies herself.

The girl is talking excitedly, still thrilled by the suggestion of a game whose rules they are establishing. Heller consents to her every request, and the scene is repeated.

Varika, with the kitten in one hand, runs down the corridor towards the radiator to reach the second basket of eggs. She picks it up, laughing, then turns towards Heller to check that he is respecting the handicap he promised her. And he waits until he sees her disappearing behind the corner that leads to the sitting room. Then he begins to move, guided by his desire like a sleepwalker.

When he reaches the sitting room, he immediately notices that the third basket on the table is missing. He moves to the exact centre of the floor and looks towards the bedroom. The door is open, the light extinguished. For a few seconds he doesn't move. It is so quiet that he thinks he can hear the purring of the cat. Every five seconds, a faint giggle from the hiding girl.

He advances, making sure that his footsteps can be heard. He stops by the door. He sees a strip of the blanket move under the bed. He turns on the light. Another giggle from the child. The last basket of eggs is missing from the chest of drawers.

'Where are you? Where have you got to?' he asks loudly. 'Where have you hidden yourself, goodness me, you've found them, all my eggs . . .'

The kitten purrs loudly in Varika's hand, as the girl looks at Heller's shoes and bites her lip to keep from laughing.

Heller opens the drawers one by one, still calling to her. He takes out the pillows, shakes the sheets, looks behind the door, then finally kneels down. He barely has time to pull back the strip of blanket before Varika slips out from her hiding place, exploding into hoarse laughter and lifting the animal clumsily into the air, as it looks around confused.

Heller, still on his knees, raises his arms in the air and concedes the game. He smiles. Varika sets the kitten on the bed and throws her arms around his neck. She slaps him on the back, celebrating her victory.

Heller strokes her hair, then gradually closes his arms around her. The little girl goes on laughing and gasping for air. If she could look him in the face right now, she would understand.

Heller glances sideways, towards the chink in the wardrobe door, then begins to squeeze.

Varika immediately stiffens.

'Let go of me,' she says.

The cat leaps away, as though it has realised that something is going on.

Varika braces her arms against Heller's shoulders, trying to pull herself away. She utters an incomprehensible word, full of consonants, with a metallic ring to it. She pushes hard to free herself, but Heller is furiously gripping her back.

He takes her head in his other hand. The door moves.

What are you doing? he thinks.

What he sees first as the door opens is Celeste's eyes. Staring, hurt, hopeless. Two pitifully faint lights in the middle of that dark frame. Then her hands. The dirty blade.

The blood.

He relaxes his grip on the little girl, who is too busy trying to save her own skin to pay any attention to what is happening in the room.

The wardrobe door flies open completely, to reveal Celeste's arms stretched out towards Heller, as though to bring him something, or take something from him.

Heller pushes the child away. She crashes into the bedside table and knocks it over, making a loud, brittle crash that petrifies the kitten on the sheets. Then he hurls himself towards Celeste.

'What have you done?' he says between pursed lips. 'What have you done?'

Only then does Varika see the scene being played out on the other side of the bed. She utters a visceral, almost masculine cry, then picks up the cat and flees from the room.

Celeste is shivering convulsively. She is still pale, but she continues to offer Heller her wounds, like a supplication. The blood is leaving her with impressive speed.

Heller grips a pillow, tears up the pillowcase to make a bandage, wraps it around Celeste's wrists and squeezes it hard. Drenching himself with blood as he picks her up and lays her out on the sheets, he realises that he is seeing everything as though through a rain-covered wind-screen.

'What have you done?' he repeats, as if there were any point. He bites at his lips until they burst.

The door banging. Varika screaming down the stairs. People coming out onto the landings. Voices asking what is going on.

Celeste's wide eyes stare at the ceiling. Her teeth chatter. Far off, she hears Heller's voice talking to someone.

'Number 31, Via dell'Addolorata. Fifth floor, Heller.'

The sound of the phone being put down.

Then nothing.

Heller hugs Celeste's head to him, and as he yields to a loud lamentation consisting of pathetic words of apology, he hears from somewhere inside himself what sounds like the roar of battle. Then he holds his breath as he plunges into that sensation.

Yes, something within him has wrought havoc, he is sure of it. It has left him with its aftermath. Something that will not outlive the dead.

Bambi

Celeste can see, now. There's her father, leaning over her. She takes his hands and looks at him. He looks unhappy.

Dad, says Celeste. How're you feeling, Dad?

He doesn't reply.

Dad. Why don't you talk to me? Are you cross with me?

He lowers his eyes as though he doesn't want to understand.

Celeste's voice cracks. She's about to cry.

Please, Dad, answer me. You never answer me.

Celeste's so tired. She covers her face with her hands, sobbing and reproducing all the suffering implied in the last word she spoke, which she repeats now like a nursery rhyme.

That's enough, now, he says after a while. Pull yourself together, dry those tears. Come on.

Yes, she says trustingly.

Yes.

Then she feels his hand behind her head.

Push, he says. Come on.

Celeste opens herself wide. She breathes in as much air as she can.

She puts her hands to her belly, then does as her father has said.

He smiles.

Then there's nothing, a breath, she's gone, she's out, she's running; no, more than that, she's gambolling, she's taking glorious long leaps, gliding down and then soaring once again to slice the air, and the birds fly up as she passes, she is light and strong, her wrists have stopped stinging, her arms and legs are slender, young and perfect, with sculpted hoofs at their ends, she can recognise things however far away they might be, everything is enormous.

It was easy, Dad.

Acknowledgements

The line 'My misery haunts me even in my dreams' spoken by Heller on p. 16 is from *The Odyssey*, Book 20, in Samuel Butler's translation (1897).

My thanks to Dalia Oggero, for the enthusiasm she always brings to my writing; Paola Gallo, for her doubts; Mimmo Scarpa, for his subtle suggestions; my brother Amleto, for Curva Sud.